WHEN COLETTE DIED

A Novel

by

L. C. Hayden

When Colette Died

A Top Publications Paperback

This edition published 1999
12221 Merit Drive, Suite 750
Dallas, Texas 75251

ISBN#: 0-9666366-6-X
Library of Congress Catalogue Card Number 99-75741

Printed in the United States of America

Acknowledgments

I would like to thank Walter J. Decker, toxicology consultant, for his advice on sleeping pills. Any errors are, of course, mine, not his. Also, a special thanks goes to gothic and mystery author Paula Paul for her tremendous suggestions and lots of kudos to those who proofread this novel: Ted Shrader, Luz Maldonado, Rich Hayden, Ray and Leslie Whiteman.

A big salute goes to the Las Vegas hit show, Legends in Concert. Without their help, I wouldn't have been able to carry this through. Jonathan (Elvis Presley) VonBrana, Susan (Marilyn Monroe) Griffith, and producer John Stuart donated their valuable time to help me gain the necessary insight into an impersonator's characteristics and motivations. Incidentally, the characters in my novel are strictly fictional and are not intended to represent anybody associated with the Legends in Concert crew.

Writing this novel, as always, was an absolute blast. I often visited Las Vegas for research purposes and met some wonderful people. Thanks to all, but especially to Sarah Bernadette, my typist and very special friend, and to my family who put up with me, especially Rich, Donald, and Robert. Rich, a big ol' hug and kiss goes to you for always willing to drive me to Las Vegas and never complaining.

Finally, a deep thanks goes to everyone associated with Top Publications, especially author and editor Bill Manchee and to my publicist Lisa A. Korth.

DEDICATION:

To Dad and Mom with lots of love
and
in loving memory of Pop and Evelyn Hayden

Chapter 1

As soon as Debbie Gunther stepped out of the limousine, she smiled, looked around, and froze.

Instinct warned her, he's here.

Somewhere among the sixty or so people who had gathered to watch her arrive, Debbie saw a figure slip behind the crowd. Just far away enough not to be recognized, yet close enough to make his presence known. Debbie felt a tingle at the back of her neck. She forced herself to ignore her growing fear.

Remembering to smile just as Colette would have done, Debbie's eyes searched the area. Her fans cheered and waved, but somewhere among them was a man who wasn't her fan. She had first noticed him three weeks ago. She was at a corner drugstore in Beverly Hills, waiting for a prescription to be refilled. She was thinking about her upcoming trip to Las Vegas when suddenly a ball hit her on the legs. She turned, expecting to see either giggling or red-faced kids. Instead, she saw a man, his back to her, turning the corner at the end of the aisle.

She dismissed the incident as only an accident, but three days later she wondered if she'd been wrong. She had been at a grocery store when someone threw a ripe tomato at her. It splattered as it hit her chest. Surprised, she looked up to see someone dashing away.

"Hey, Colette!" a fan cheered.

Debbie blinked away the memory, turned to her fans,

smiled, and waved. She wasn't about to let him ruin this day. Today, she'd concentrate on being Colette. It almost worked. She had pushed the thought away when just beyond the crowd, she spotted him again. Immediately, he slid behind some columns.

That's the way it always was. Every time she saw him, he managed to dart past her view. A second later, after she looked away, she knew he was there again. Just as she knew he was out there now. Waiting. Watching. He was obviously playing some kind of a hideous game with rules he alone understood.

Fear nipped at the edges of Debbie's nerves. She looked around and felt relief when she spotted the two casino security guards. They flanked the frosted, gold-plated doors of the Crystal Palace Casino. Maybe she should talk to them about this man who's following her. She'd tell them how she saw him first at the Los Angeles airport and now here in Las Vegas. She could do that, but what could they do?

It'd be better if she told someone she trusted. But who? The truth was she didn't have anyone to tell.

Still beaming what she hoped looked like a smile full of confidence, she made her way toward the casino's entrance. The two guards held the crowd back as Debbie walked toward the casino's doors.

A young man, wearing the dusty blue and silver casino uniform, held the front door open. His right hand made a sweeping motion, inviting her to step into the Crystal Palace Casino.

Debbie turned to the crowd, raised her head high, and continued to wave. She forced her fears into the recesses of her mind. She stepped inside and enjoyed the casino's cool air, the tinkling of coins dropping, the jingle-jangle of the slot machines, and the sounds of people having fun.

She concentrated on the casino's stately entrance. Its polished blue and white marble, gilded woodwork, and glittering chandeliers all competed for her attention.

To her left a slowly revolving carousel, overhung with gigantic pieces of glittering glass which resembled different-sized crystals, immediately caught her eye. A change girl, dressed in the usual dusty blue and silver uniform, handed a young couple a red tray filled with dollar coins. Debbie noticed that mostly young adults played the machines in the carousel.

Several players momentarily forgot their machines and stared at Debbie in awe. She knew that she really did resemble Colette, the famous movie star who had so tragically been murdered in this same casino. It hardly seemed possible that five years had already passed since that meaningless act had been performed.

Debbie was suddenly gripped by the sensation that she didn't belong here. Colette had belonged. But Debbie knew she lacked Colette's confidence, her easy grace, her devil-may-care detachment. It was best, she knew, not to think about those things. She forced herself to look at the people who had waited for her.

She smiled broadly, wrinkled her nose, and winked, just as Colette would have done.

"Miss Debbie Gunther."

Debbie turned at the sound of her name and faced two men. The one to her right spoke first. "I'm Jack Armstrong," he said. "Welcome to Las Vegas." He extended his hand.

Debbie shook it and noted that his strong, firm grasp matched his healthy-looking physique. Although in his late thirties or early forties, he still had his youthful, sturdy body. His dark, wavy hair and pale-green bedroom eyes hypnotize those around him. His suit matched the casino's colors.

Jack pointed to the man standing beside him. He wore jeans and an open-neck white short sleeve shirt. "Miss Gunther, this is Bill Davis, your director."

Debbie forced a smile. Although she tried not to, she felt herself shrink back, just a little. Something about the director--perhaps his powerful, broad shoulder--intimidated her. "I know you," she said. "We've talked several times on the phone." She extended her hand. "Please call me Debbie."

Bill clasped Debbie's hand a little bit too long, too hard. His eyes traveled down to her breasts, and he made no attempt to hide it. "You are very pretty, Debbie, and the resemblance is remarkable." His eyes momentarily took on a deep-set hollow look. "If I didn't know better, I'd swear you were Colette. Tell me, are you nervous?"

"About impersonating Colette?"

Bill nodded.

"I'm petrified. But I'll do my best to bring Colette alive for the audience." Again she wrinkled her nose and winked.

"Good. I'm glad to hear that. Now, go freshen up and in about an hour, meet me on stage, so we can go over your act--unless, of course, you're busy with the interview."

A group of people rudely walked between them. Debbie waited until they disappeared before asking, "What interview?"

"We've arranged for you to meet with Dan Springer," Jack said. "He's the top reporter for *Star World Magazine*. What he writes about you will determine the success of our show. But I'm sure that won't be a problem. Your charming ways will completely captivate him." He smiled and winked at Debbie, setting her at ease. "Naturally, it would be to both of our advantages if the story was favorable."

"I'll do my best," Debbie promised.

"Good! I knew we could count on you." He turned toward Bill. "Didn't I tell you, Bill, that she'd be wonderful? I've just had that feeling ever since the first time I saw her perform."

A change girl, an attractive lady in her early twenties wearing a short, sparkling blue skirt and frilly, white blouse laced with silver trim, approached them. "Excuse me, Miss Gunther, I have a message for you." She handed her an envelope and left.

Debbie glanced at it and noticed her name was written

in plain block letters. She searched her mind, trying to come up with the name of someone who knew she was in Las Vegas. Several co-workers and friends from Los Angeles knew she was here, but she wasn't close enough to any of them to keep in touch with them. That only left one person: the man who followed her to Las Vegas. Unable to stop herself, she ripped the envelope open.

The message, like her name on the envelope, was written in plain block letters. It read: DEBBIE, WATCH FOR ME ON OPENING NIGHT--AND REMEMBER COLETTE. She turned the note over. It was unsigned. She stared at the note, trying to make sense of it.

"Anything wrong?" Jack's eyebrows furrowed. "Bad news?"

"Uh, oh, no," she stuttered. "Just a note from a fan." She smiled and stuffed the note inside her purse. Later she'd deal with it. Now she needed to concentrate on being Colette.

"In that case," Jack said, "we'll let you go up to your suite. I'll drop by later to make sure the accommodations are to your liking." He signaled for the bellboy who moments ago had arrived and stood just beyond hearing range.

"Show Ms. Gunther to her suite," Jack told the bellboy.

"Yes, sir, Mr. Armstrong."

The way he answered--whether out of respect or fear--made Debbie immediately realize that Jack Armstrong was not a man to fool with.

She watched Jack and Bill walk down the aisle between a row of blackjack tables. They stopped at a twenty-one table and observed the action for a while. Debbie turned her attention to the bellboy. "Don't I need to register first?"

"No, ma'am. Mr. Armstrong said that everything has been taken care of. All we need is a signature, and we'll send the card to your room," he said.

Debbie nodded and followed him. She hadn't taken more than a few steps when that strange sensation overtook her. Someone was watching her. She could feel the eyes analyzing her once again. She stopped and slowly turned.

She'd been right. She spotted not only one pair of eyes staring at her, but several pairs. They were envious eyes, inquisitive eyes, awed eyes--but none were the eyes she was looking for.

She had obviously let her imagination get carried away. That man who had tormented her in California was still there. This was Nevada. What would make her think he had followed her here? She remembered the note inside her purse.

She swallowed hard, smiled, and waved at the people. Then she hurried to catch up with the bellboy.

* * * *

One specific pair of eyes would have interested Debbie had she noticed them. They were there when she first stepped into the casino. They were there when she waved to the people. They were there because they were waiting. Waiting for the right moment.

The eyes were narrow and smoldering, the brows level. The gaze was direct, cold, hard, and filled with anger.

Chapter 2

Debbie waited until she was in her suite before she retrieved the crumpled note from her purse. Prior to arriving in Las Vegas, she had convinced herself that no one was following her. But now, now--

She wrinkled the note with a force which startled her. She stared at it, then straightened it out. It didn't mean anything. There was just some nut out there--

Like the nut who murdered Colette five years ago?

A chill covered Debbie's body. She shook her head, trying to force out the growing feeling of panic that was gnawing at her.

The abruptness of the knock on the door startled her. She hesitated for a second, then remembered the bellboy and her luggage. She opened the door a crack and a woman in her mid-forties, with mostly gray hair and a few golden strands, smiled at her. "Debbie Gunther?"

Debbie cautiously opened the door the rest of the way. "May I help you?"

"My, my, my! I can't believe how much you look like Colette. I swear, child, you are Colette's twin," the woman said, stepping inside, almost pushing Debbie out of the way.

"It's my job to look like Colette," Debbie answered, not quite sure what to make of this woman. "I'm Debbie Gunther, and you?"

"Oh, I'm Ann Thompson, but you can call me Annie." She sat down on the plush sofa.

"Annie? Like Colette's Annie?"

There was a slight smile. "I guess you could say that."

"This is indeed a pleasure. I've read so much about you. Have you retired?"

"No, in fact, I'm working here in the casino. After Colette died, Ms. Elizabeth offered to take me in. She said I'd work for only the celebrities, the V.I.P.'s. That's why I'm here. I'll be your personal maid, and my first official duty is to bring you the registration form. It needs your signature."

"Thank you very much." Debbie reached for it.

"Have you had a chance to meet Ms. Elizabeth?"

"Who?"

"Elizabeth Lovingsworth. You know, your boss. She owns this place. You do know who I'm talking about."

Debbie nodded. She had heard of Ms. Lovingsworth-- who hadn't?--but she had never met her.

"Anyway, like I was saying, Colette would always confide in me, so if you want to know anything about Colette-- anything at all--you come to me. You hear?"

"Thank you, Annie. That's very kind of you."

Annie smiled and nodded. "Well, if it helps your career, I'll be glad to fill you in. You just keep that in mind." She patted the couch. "Nice, very soft."

Debbie nodded. "Yes, it is. I'm properly impressed."

Again, Annie smiled and stood up. "I best be going. Ms. Elizabeth runs a very tight ship, and she wouldn't approve of me sitting here, talking to you."

"I won't tell," Debbie said, smiling and winking at Annie.

"You're all right, kid," Annie said and glanced toward the kitchen. "There's plenty of fresh fruits. I made sure of that. What about the refrigerator? Does it have everything you like?"

"As long as there's plenty of orange juice, I'll be fine. I always drink a big, tall glass before I go to bed. Thanks for asking."

"It's strictly my pleasure," Annie said. "Now if you could just sign the registration form, I'll deliver it for you."

* * *

As Annie waited for the elevator to take her back downstairs, she clenched her fist and struck the air above her. She celebrated her first small victory.

Chapter 3

Debbie stood in front of the stage which consisted of a false front of a life-like, low-income housing project. She admired its intricate detail then turned to face the empty showroom. In a little over a month, the stage's curtain would rise. She'd be standing where she was now, except that by then, she'd be the star of the show. She'd awed the audience into believing that they were actually watching Colette.

She stood staring at the dark showroom, her mind filling it with enthusiastic fans. Many people would--

A movement in the shadows caught her attention. She studied the area carefully, but even as her eyes adjusted to the dim light, she couldn't make anything out. It must had been her imagination. She shrugged. One of the things she could do to improve her show was to--

Firm fingers grabbed her shoulder.

Debbie threw her arms outward and turned as fast as she could. Her extended arms hit someone.

"Ouch," he said.

"Who the hell are you?" she screamed.

"Gee, I'm sorry," said the embarrassed teenager. His face bore the evidence of a heavy case of acne. "I've been calling your name, and I swear you were staring straight at me. I was sure you'd seen me." He clutched a large, white box protectively in front of him.

Feeling awkward, Debbie smiled self-consciously. "You scared me half to death."

The youth looked down, obviously embarrassed.

Debbie quickly added, "I'm sorry too. I was just lost in thought, and I really didn't see you coming."

The young man smiled shyly and looked away. He shifted his weight from one foot to the other. "Gee, you're really, uh, beautiful. If I didn't know better, I'd swear you're... you're..." He looked up at Debbie and shrugged.

"Colette?" she said.

Obviously relieved that he hadn't offended Debbie, his head bobbed up and down. "Could I please have your autograph?"

"I'd be honored," Debbie said.

He set the box down and searched his pockets for a piece of paper and a pen. When he realized he didn't have any, he shrugged.

"Why don't you follow me backstage? My director has a box full of publicity pictures. How about if I autograph one of those for you?"

His face brightened. "You'd do that? Yeah, I'd love one of those!" He started walking and tripped over the box. "Oh, gosh, I almost forgot." He picked up the package and handed it to her. "It's for you."

Debbie sucked in her breath. She had never had a fan give her a gift.

As though reading her thoughts the teenager quickly added, "Oh, it's not from me. It's from Ms. Elizabeth."

The shock Debbie felt was even larger now than when she thought the gift came from this young stranger. "Ms. Lovingsworth?" Debbie asked whispering the name.

"Ms. Elizabeth."

"What?"

"She likes to be called Ms. Elizabeth."

Debbie nodded and filed that information away. She accepted the box. "Let's go back to Bill's office."

As she led the way across the stage, she heard a man

call her. Debbie turned and caught a glimpse of him as he headed toward her. She took him in from his shoes to the top of his head. She saw a distinguished looking man in his late twenties or early thirties. He had ice blue eyes and jet black hair.

As he hurried toward her, she tilted her head so that her hair fell seductively across her right eye.

"Hi, I'm Dan Springer, the reporter from *Star World Magazine*." He put his hand out to shake hers.

Debbie accepted it and took a step closer. The touch of his hand sent a tingling sensation through her body.

"Your hair looks beautiful," he said. He reached out to fix a wayward lock.

"Thank you. It's a pleasure to meet you." She inhaled deeply. She felt breathless. She wanted him to reach out again and touch her hair, her face. She wanted to feel that electricity again. She had never felt this way just after meeting someone. She looked at him and his eyes smiled.

The delivery boy cleared his throat, and the magic was gone.

Debbie said, "I promised this young man an autographed picture, and we were on our way up to Bill's office to get it. Would you care to join us?"

"That's fine," he said. "Let me get that box for you."

Debbie nodded and marveled at the idea that chivalry wasn't completely dead. She handed it to him. "Thanks." She led them to Bill Davis' office, a room jammed with two large desks, a bookcase filled with more papers than books, and three plush, swivel chairs. On the wall beside the door was a sixteen by twenty color picture of Colette. It was signed, "With all my love, Colette."

"About two weeks ago when I was talking to Bill on the phone, he told me that the pictures had just arrived." Debbie looked around the room. "Now, where could he have put them?" She hoped she didn't have to dig through his drawers.

She spotted a box on the second bookshelf directly in front of her. She pulled the box from the shelf, placed it on Bill's desk, and opened it. "Ah, there they are," she said. She picked up a picture and a pen. She turned to the teenager. "What's your name?"

"Mike Logan."

She signed the picture. "Here you are, Mike." She handed it to him. "Drop by sometime, and I'll give you a tip for delivering that box."

The teenager's face reddened. "Oh, no, thank you. That won't be necessary. The picture is enough." He smiled awkwardly, started to leave, but suddenly stopped. "I almost forgot." He said. "You're supposed to wear that on opening night." He pointed to the box. "I mean the dress. It's from Ms. Elizabeth."

Debbie wrinkled her nose--a gesture which had once been Colette's trademark--and smiled. "Hope it fits then."

After the teenager left, Debbie turned her attention to Dan. "This is my director's office." She looked for a comfortable place to conduct the interview. The office was large, but it was so jammed packed that there was hardly any room to move around. "There's no real place to get comfortable. Why don't we go up to my suite?"

"Sounds good to me," Dan said. Without asking, he picked up the box and carried it for Debbie.

When they entered her suite, Dan let out a whistle. He set the box on the couch. "Wow! I always wanted to know how the movie stars lived. This is really gorgeous," he said eyeing the crystal knick knacks.

"I'm rather impressed myself," Debbie answered. "Believe me, I've lived with this type of V.I.P. treatment for a while, but nothing this fancy. It's like this is too much. It should be reserved for a real V.I.P." *Like Colette*.

"Fascinating bit of information," he said. "That's the kind of stuff I want to capture in my story." He reached into his shirt pocket and produced a small writing pad and a mechanical pencil. "Let's start with the usual background stuff," he said. "Tell me about your mother."

A veil of sadness descended on her. Her mother. What had she been like? She sighed. "I never knew her. She died during childbirth." And silently she added, and my father never forgave me for killing her.

She could still remember the harsh words her father often repeated to her, "I'll never let you forget that you're the reason why your mama is dead." He pointed an accusing finger at her.

Debbie looked down at her hands. So much had changed since then. She looked back up at Dan.

"So you were raised by your father?"

"Sort of. For the first eight years I lived with my maternal grandparents. Then my father came for me." Bitterness swept through Debbie. The only reason her father had come for her was because Grandma was tired of taking care of her. When Grandma called demanding he take Debbie back, he refused. Grandma then threatened him with a child neglect lawsuit if he didn't show up.

Dan's voice brought her back to the present.

"Are you two close?" he asked.

"Not really. By the time I went to live with him, most of my early childhood was gone. That's where most of the memories are made." She swallowed, remembering the agonizing pain of her childhood memories. With clear, haunting images she recalled the day her father had come to pick her up. He had stared at Grandma and with the warmth of a glacier had said, "I want you to know, Mrs. Dolan, that I don't give a damn about your granddaughter. But just to put your mind at ease--although I know you couldn't care less--I'll promise you that I'll feed her and buy her clothes. But I will never love her."

Never love her.

No one's ever loved me.

At a time when other children were out playing, Debbie was inside the house, cleaning, sweeping, cooking, sewing. She had to prove to Grandma that she was somebody and not as Grandma said, "An insignificant speck of dust."

But it seemed to Debbie that no matter how hard she tried, no matter how hard she worked, Debbie remained a nobody.

One day when she was particularly tired, Grandma found a streak of dust Debbie had missed. Debbie cringed, waiting for the crack of the whip. Instead, Grandma stared at her, then went to the phone to call her father. "Pick her up. I've had her for eight years, it's your turn now. I don't want her."

Father hadn't wanted her either.

And Debbie had remained a nobody until Colette entered her life.

"Tell me," Dan said, "how you started impersonating Colette."

Debbie smiled. "I have my choir teacher to thank for that. It was my junior year and her name was Mrs. Kathy--that's with a *K*--Genes."

"Was she the one who suggested you should impersonate Colette?"

"In a round-about way, yes. You see, when I was in high school, I was an awkward teenager. You know the type: sloppy dresser, always hunching down, absolutely no grace, very awkward."

"That's very hard to believe. You're the essence of perfection."

Startled, Debbie felt the blood rush to her face. He smiled, and his eyes were gentle and warm. That only made her blush some more. She was probably still in high school the last time someone made her blush, and here she was, blushing like a school girl again. "Well, I was," she said, trying to cover her embarrassment. "Mrs. Genes kept telling me I reminded her of someone and that I had a beautiful voice."

"But you didn't believe her?"

Debbie shook her head. "She made me stay after school one day to audition for her."

"How did that turn out?"

"At first, horrible. She asked me who I listened to. I told her Colette. Everybody was listening to Colette. She asked me if I knew 'I'm Full of Life?' I told her, yes, everyone knew that song."

"So you sang it?"

"Yeah, but you should have heard me." She smiled and shook her head at the memory. "Mrs. Genes played the introductory notes on the piano, but I missed the cue. Without saying a word, she began over again.

"This time I sang, but my voice was weak and timid. I held on to the edge of the piano. Then something snapped, and my need to hold on vanished. My voice became strong and powerful. By the time the song was over, I found my body swaying to the beat of the song. Mrs. Genes said I was terrific. Then she told me that's who I reminded her of: Colette."

"And the rest is history," Dan said.

"I suppose you could say that. I started studying Colette's tapes, becoming more and more like her until it became second nature." For the first time, Debbie felt the hope which had up to now managed to evade her. The ugly duckling could turn into a swan. She said good-bye to Debbie, the nobody, and hello to Debbie, the impersonator, the fan of Colette, the woman everyone loved.

"That's why Colette is so important to me," Debbie said. "She opened a whole new world for me. I just wish I could repay her somehow, but since she's dead, I know I can't. So I'm doing this instead. I'm impersonating her and, hopefully, honoring her." She felt foolish and very much unsophisticated. She noticed that Dan was staring at her with a full-blown smile.

"Kinda dumb, eh?" Debbie asked.

Dan shook his head. "Not at all. You're so refreshingly open. I wish every movie star was like you."

For the second time today, Debbie felt herself blush. She decided to change the subject. "Where are my manners? What would you care to drink?" She eyed the box resting on the couch next to Dan.

"Do you have any beer?"

"Sure do." She headed toward the kitchen, opened the refrigerator and poured Dan a tall glass of ice-cold Michelob. For herself, after careful consideration, she chose a glass of Dom Perignon. Maybe now Dan would think she was sophisticated. She returned to the den carrying both drinks. She handed him his beer. As he reached for it, Debbie noticed that he wasn't wearing a wedding band.

It had been quite a while since she had looked at a man's hand in order to check his marital status. She wondered why she had done so, then dismissing the thought, she raised her glass in a salute to the interview.

Dan did the same and took a small sip. "Tell me a little about Debbie, then we'll talk about Colette." He set his glass down.

Debbie considered this for a minute, then eyeing the box resting next to Dan, she answered, "Well, for one thing, Debbie's curious."

"Meaning?"

Debbie stood up and picked up the box. "Ms. Elizabeth sent me this. She wants me to wear it on opening night. Would you mind if I take a peek?" Debbie felt somewhat embarrassed at her obvious curiosity.

Dan raised his eyebrows in surprise, then smiled reassuringly. "Sure. I'm in no hurry."

"This won't take long," she said as she removed the ribbons off the box. As she undid the last tape, she smiled triumphantly. "Ready?" she asked, holding her breath in anticipation. "Here it goes!" She opened the box and peeked inside. Immediately, she backed away a pace, as though she'd been punched full in the face.

With numbed shock, she raised her eyes to meet Dan's.

Chapter 4

The Boss stared at the middle drawer, wondering if it was safe to open. Down on the bottom, the article which had been placed there five years ago was buried underneath all of the official-looking papers.

For five long years the secret had remained there. Undisturbed. But now Debbie Gunther was here. Feeling a certain amount of contempt, the Boss opened the drawer, shuffled through the papers, dug out the article, and began to read:

> LAS VEGAS (AP)--World famous actress and singer, Colette, 25, was fatally wounded while performing last night on stage in Las Vegas' Crystal Palace Casino.
>
> The alleged assassin, Sam Capacini, 43, was also killed by a Crystal Palace security guard, Edward Gonzalez.
>
> According to Gonzalez, Capacini, who had no previous criminal record, gunned down Colette because God had ordered him to.

The Boss set the article down. There was no use reading the rest.

Sam Capacini. That pathetic retard...

* * *

Sam had agreed to meet the Boss by the park bench

under the elm tree. When he arrived, he found the Boss casually reading the newspaper.

Sam sat on the opposite end of the bench and called out to the Boss. Immediately the newspaper was disregarded, neatly folded and placed on the bench between them. "I'm sorry about your cancer," the Boss said.

Sam sighed. "I don't want to die." He looked past the Boss, toward the birds singing in the trees. "I'm afraid."

"Then live, Sam."

The command had been given with such force that Sam's attention was drawn back toward the Boss. "How?" he asked after a long pause.

"Take what's yours, Sam." The Boss leaned forward, emphasizing the point being made with an outstretched index finger. "Take a life."

"I...I don't understand."

"All you got to do is buy someone's life."

The statement hit Sam like an arrow piercing the middle of his stomach. He found it hard to breathe. "Can you really do that?" Sam bit his lower lip as he waited for the answer.

"Sure!" The Boss raised a hand and waved it as though implying this happens every day. "If you buy someone's life who is young enough and vital, then all those years that person had left, simply go to you."

Sam stared at the Boss, wishing he was smart, like the Boss. "I never knew you could do that."

"Very few people know that." The Boss leaned back on the park bench and with both index fingers formed a steeple. "In fact, the only people who know this are the smart ones. You do want to be smart, don't you?"

Oh, yes. Sam had always wanted to be smart. Then nobody would ever tease him again. Or laugh at him. He nodded.

"That's what I thought," the Boss said. "That's why I told you. Now you're one of the smart ones--but you must promise me that you will never tell anyone I told you. We, the smart people, just know certain things and we never discuss them. And if you do, people will know right away you're not one of the smart ones. You wouldn't want that to happen."

Sam shook his head. He felt better already, now that he was smart. But even though he knew that Secret, something still bothered him. He hoped the Boss wouldn't mind if he asked a simple question. "How do you buy a life?"

"With a gun."

Sam gasped. "You...you shoot them?"

"Yes, of course, how else can their years become yours?"

Sam was quiet for a minute. "But who do you kill?"

"The one person who represents life the most."

"Who's that?"

The Boss shrugged and picked up the discarded newspaper. "Think about it. The answer must come from you. It must be someone very young, someone whom everybody recognizes as being full of life." The Boss' attention turned to the newspaper.

Sam desperately wished that he could come up with a name. He looked around Waltman Park, hoping somehow to find a hidden answer.

The Boss once again folded the newspaper and placed it between them. Sam glanced at it. There was a big picture of Colette, advertising her opening night at the Crystal Palace Casino. Her picture had been circled with bright red ink, drawing his attention to the advertisement.

She sure was beautiful. And young. And full of life.

Sam felt pleased. The Boss was right. He *was* smart now. He had come up with a name all by himself. "Colette," he said and smiled triumphantly.

"Excellent choice," the Boss said.

* * *

There had been many sessions after this one, all at

Waltman Park, all to work out the details. And when it was all over, the Boss felt pleased.

Less than twenty-four hours after Colette was murdered, her albums and her poster sales had exceeded all records. She was on her way to becoming a legend.

As for Sam--poor Sam, he had to die. There was no other way around it. For years to come people would speculate what went through his mind, but because he was dead, he took the secret of Colette's death with him.

Now only one person knew the truth--the mastermind behind it all. And certainly the secret would always be safe.

The perfect murder had been committed.

Chapter 5

"How could she?" Debbie fumed. "Of all the inconsiderate, thoughtless things--" She pointed to the box. "This tops it all." She started to pick up the red-sequined dress then quickly pulled back her hands at the thought of having to touch it. "She died in a dress just like this one. I can't possibly wear it. This is sick. You know that? Really sick."

"I agree," Dan said. "There is such a thing as too perfect an imitation. What are you going to do about it?"

Debbie stood up and began to pace. "I don't know, but I can't possibly wear it. If I did, it's like I'm dirtying Colette's image. And I could never do that to her." She spread out her hands in the front of her and shook her head. "I'm going to go talk to Ms. Elizabeth. Would you mind if we continue our interview later?"

Dan stood up. "I do have a deadline. Any possibility of meeting later on today?"

Debbie remembered that he wasn't wearing a wedding band. It wouldn't hurt to be a little bold. "I'm afraid I'm pretty busy. The only time I'm not booked is for supper. Maybe you'd like to join me then--that is, of course, if your wife wouldn't mind."

Agonized eyes stared at Debbie, but a second later the look was gone. "There is no Mrs. Springer." His voice strangled on the words. He closed his note pad and put his mechanical pencil back in his shirt pocket. "What time is supper?" His forced cheeriness was obvious.

"About seven."

"Where?"

"Meet me here, and we'll decide where to go."

Dan nodded and headed toward the door. Debbie walked beside him. "Good luck with Ms. Elizabeth," he said.

"Thank you. I haven't met her yet, and I'm a bit nervous."

"Don't be. You've got a legitimate gripe, and she's a fair woman."

"You know her?"

"I did a story on her. From what I gathered, she's the type of person who commands respect from others, and she gets that respect by treating people fairly. She'll listen to you-- especially if you point out that the audience would be turned off. Remind her that the word travels fast, and it wouldn't take too long before the show is a flop. If that's the case, then the casino will lose money, not only from lost income on the tickets, but also from the people who would have stayed to gamble after the show. If you put it to her on those terms, I'm sure she'll see your side of it." He winked, smiled, and raised his thumb up, signifying victory.

Then he was gone and Debbie stood at the door, watching him until he turned the corner at the end of the hall.

Chapter 6

"I understand congratulations are in order."

Jack turned at the sound of Elizabeth's voice. All around him the jingle of money being dropped in the slot machines reverberated. "Why is that?" he asked.

"I have never known you to be modest." Elizabeth headed away from the row of slot machines containing computerized graphics and toward the gaming tables. Jack walked beside her.

"You're talking about my finding the fake stack of chips." Jack glanced to his right at the crystal-shaped bar. Four people were sitting, sipping drinks, but only one was playing the video poker machine recessed into the counter top. Jack made a mental note to plant someone at those machines in order to draw more customers to them.

"Tell me about it," Elizabeth said.

"During one of my unscheduled rounds I noticed that Harold was--"

"Harold?"

"The ex-croupier in that pit." Jack pointed with his head.

Elizabeth nodded.

"I noticed that he seemed rather tense whenever I was around. Then I saw the two hustlers quickly heading away from him. I was sure they had just finished talking. Figuring out what was going on wasn't hard."

"Congratulations," Elizabeth said, "your powers of observation has just earned you the use of the 'Gold Pencil'--

you're now free to grant anyone you choose free room, food, and air fare."

Although Jack felt his face beam like a lighthouse, he did his best to maintain his composure. "What about Thomas Buller?"

"What about him? Do you want to know if he also has the 'Gold Pencil' power? No, he doesn't." As they walked past the shift bosses, pit bosses, floorwalker, dealer, and croupiers in the various pits, Jack and Elizabeth made sure that they were seen. Doing unscheduled rounds like this always made it more difficult for any potential traitor to carry on his schemes of skimming from table winnings.

Elizabeth continued, "But that doesn't mean that you'll automatically become the general manager. I'm still considering Thomas for that position."

"I realize that," Jack said. "But I do want you to know that I've worked very hard for that position."

"So has Thomas."

Off to their left a woman screamed. Elizabeth and Jack stopped their rounds and turned toward the lady. Within seconds, the change lady was standing beside her, congratulating her for winning three-thousand dollars.

Security came and informed her that the machine would pay her the first $400 in coins. She would receive the rest in cash as soon as she provided proof of her social security number. In the meantime, the machine continued to pound out the casino's snappy tune, signifying a winner.

By now a small crowd had gathered to watch the lucky gambler. They too wanted to win, and that was good for business. After letting the machine ring for several minutes, the floor manager turned it off, and some of the people who had gathered to watch started dropping their coins in adjacent machines.

"It seems to me," Elizabeth said resuming their rounds, "that the one who does the most for the casino will get that position."

"I'm working on something special right now," Jack said.

"I assumed as much. Tell me, does it involve Debbie Gunther?"

Jack loosened his tie and cleared his throat.

"So it does," Elizabeth said. "I was afraid of that."

Jack was unsure as to how to answer her. He noticed a security guard heading toward them and thanked his lucky stars. Jack pointed him out.

"Hello, Ms. Elizabeth, Mr. Armstrong," the security officer said. "I got a message for you. Ms. Debbie Gunther wishes to speak to you."

"Tell her to meet me in my office in ten minutes." After the security guard left, Elizabeth turned to Jack. "Good luck with your scheme, and if you know what's good for you, it better not backfire. Otherwise..." She shrugged and walked away.

Chapter 7

Even before Debbie stepped all the way into the office, she noticed that Elizabeth, a striking, tall, slim woman in her mid-thirties, was already coming around her desk. Elizabeth's hand was outstretched, and a wide smile was plastered on her face.

Suddenly Elizabeth stopped, her smile slowly fading like a vanishing mirage. "Colette," she whispered. All color drained from her face.

Debbie smiled. "No, actually Debbie Gunther."

Elizabeth shook herself. "Yes, of course. Excuse me; I'm normally not this rude. It's just that I expected you to look like her on stage, but not all of the time." She eyed the long box under Debbie's arm.

"To be truthful, I do have to tint my hair to match Colette's. Her hair was a lot blonder than mine."

"Only your hairdresser knows for sure," Elizabeth said, analyzing Debbie's hair. "Come, let's get acquainted." She led Debbie to one of the two leather couches in the reception area of her office. "We'll be more comfortable here."

Debbie quickly glanced around the room. It was a stylish office decorated in various shades of the casino's predominate colors: pale blue and silver. Soft, indirect lighting provided a comfortable atmosphere. Debbie set the box down on one of the armchairs and sat down.

"Colette's favorite was Mai Tai." Elizabeth was already behind the wet bar, preparing two drinks. "Ever had one?"

"I attended a Hawaiian-themed party. I had some then."

"Did you like them?"

"I enjoyed them." She noticed the office had three operating TV's. One showed a cashier ringing up some money at one of the casino's stores. The second one displayed a blackjack table in action. The third screen focused on a row of one-arm bandits. Several people carrying buckets of money stood in front of the machines dropping three five-dollar tokens at one time.

"Good. I'll make us some then." A few minutes later, Elizabeth set a tall glass on the crystal coffee table in front of Debbie. "I'm sorry that I haven't stopped by to meet you, but I trust Jack made suitable arrangements."

"Oh, yes, very nice." She took a sip. It was a bit too strong for her taste. "Delicious," she said.

Elizabeth nodded and walked over to her desk. On its upper left-hand corner was a control panel. She pushed the first three buttons. Immediately the panels on the TV screen changed. Now they displayed one of the hotel's corridors, the baccarat table, and a cashier at the coffee shop. "That's part of my job," Elizabeth said. "I have to keep an eye on everything that happens here--especially since I'm a woman. I feel that I have to prove myself constantly in this men's world."

"It must be hard."

"Sometimes, but you do what you must. Right now I have to show everyone I can carry on, even without my father's help." Elizabeth walked away from her desk and sat on one of the soft armchairs. "My father used to run this hotel, but ever since his stroke--six years ago--his health has deteriorated, and I've pretty much taken over."

"I admire you for that," Debbie said. "Where's your father now?"

"He has his own suite here in the hotel, but he hardly leaves it. He conducts most of his business from his bed."

Elizabeth took one large gulp, then set the glass down. "So much about me. Now tell me about you."

"Not much to say. I enjoy what I do, and I have a great deal of respect for Colette, which is why I'd like to talk to you about the gift."

"What gift?"

The question took Debbie by surprise. She pointed to the box. "The dress."

"What dress?"

Debbie reached for the box and opened it. "This dress," she said partially taking it out of the box.

The sequins caught the sun's rays shining through the window, momentarily blinding Elizabeth. When Elizabeth realized what it was, she let out a gasp. "Where did you get that?"

"You sent it to me," Debbie said, closing the box. She saw that Elizabeth was staring at her with a blank expression that urged her to add, "Didn't you?"

Elizabeth vehemently shook her head.

"The delivery boy said you told him that I was to wear that dress for my opening performance."

"What delivery boy?"

"I don't know. One of the casino runners, I suppose."

"Men look at women. Even women look at women. We hire only women to be casino runners." Elizabeth picked up the dress. "Do you remember what he looked like? Did you get his name--anything?"

"He was young, a teenager, maybe--or in his early twenties." Damn, if she hadn't been so mesmerized by Dan... "Dan was there. Maybe he'll remember something else."

"Dan Springer? The reporter?"

Debbie nodded. "He came to interview me. He arrived just in time for the autograph." Debbie stopped-the autograph! Of course! She had written his name. It was...uh... "Logan!" What was his first name? She had always been terrible at remembering names. She threw her arms up in despair. "I'm sorry, That's not much to go on. His last is Logan and his first name begins with a letter in the middle of the alphabet. Mark, Larry, Mike. Something like that."

Elizabeth stood up, walked over to her desk and picked up the phone. "CP 3A." She waited for an answer.

Debbie listened intently, trying to figure out whose code CP 3A belonged to. Nothing that Elizabeth said gave her a clue.

Elizabeth continued, "Get to the files and pull the one on Logan. Male, possibly in his early twenties. I want it ASAP." After she replaced the phone, her hand lingered on it. Her eyebrows were furrowed in obviously deep concentration.

When Debbie looked back up, Elizabeth said, "Now while we wait to talk to this Logan character, I want you to tell me the entire story without leaving the smallest of details out."

After Debbie finished with her narration, Elizabeth stood up, walked over to the window and stared at the reddening desert sun. Her arms were crossed, her finger idly drumming on her arms.

There came a knock on the door, but Elizabeth continued to stare. Debbie wondered if she should mention anything. Just as Debbie decided that she should, Elizabeth said in a voice loud enough to be heard through the closed door, "CP 3A?"

"Yes," a male voice behind the door answered.

Elizabeth walked around her desk and stood by Debbie. "Come in," she said.

Debbie was surprised to see Jack Armstrong.

He apparently didn't notice her as he immediately began addressing Elizabeth. "Are you sure on that name? I--" He abruptly stopped when he saw Debbie. Suddenly, his face wrinkled in alarm. "Debbie! I thought you had already left. Ms. Elizabeth, is something wrong?"

"The file, Jack. Where is the damn file?" Although

Elizabeth's voice was low and smooth, Debbie could detect a fine line of anger edging into her tone.

"Crystal Palace doesn't have a single employee by the name of Logan."

"What about the back files? Did you check those?"

"Two Logans. Jonathan Logan worked last year for three months. He was fired when--" Jack glanced at Debbie as though wondering if he should continue. He shrugged and decided to go on, "--when the casino keno game hit the big prize of seven-hundred twenty-five thousand dollars."

"Why was he fired?"

"Standard casino rule. Chances of anyone winning big like that are so small, someone must have cheated. Rather than wasting money finding out who it was, we fired everyone. It was easier."

"It makes sense. What else do we know about him?"

"He was forty-two and black."

"The other Logan."

"Female, fifty-one, cleaning lady, rest rooms, main casino floor, employed for three years. Quit because of health problems four years ago."

"No other Logans?"

Jack shook his head.

Elizabeth turned to stare at Debbie. If Elizabeth was trying to make Debbie feel like a six-year old child waiting to be punished, she was certainly doing an outstanding job. "I may be wrong," Debbie said, "but I was sure his last name was Logan."

"What did he look like?" Elizabeth asked.

"His most distinguished feature was his face. It was covered with pimples."

"Pimples?" Elizabeth looked appalled. "A face like that would offend our customers. We'd never hire someone with pimples all over his face." She turned to Jack. "Get on this immediately and by tomorrow morning, I expect an answer."

"I'll get right on it," Jack said. "I'm looking for a Logan--is that it?"

"Tell him," Elizabeth said, turning to Debbie.

"Someone sent me Colette's death dress, claiming it came from Ms. Elizabeth." Debbie opened the box and for the first time, took the dress completely out.

The front of the formal looked just like it had before Colette died, but it was the back of the dress which attracted Elizabeth's attention. She gasped and yanked it out of Debbie's hand. Her color drained from her face and her normally bright green eyes lost all expression. "My God, it can't be!"

Jack took a step closer. Debbie held her breath.

"Don't you see it?" Elizabeth's voice was unusually high. "Right here. Look." She pointed to a small rip in the back of the dress. "When Colette was shot, she fell backwards, hitting the stool. Her dress got caught and ripped--just like this."

Debbie felt her throat tighten and she could feel Elizabeth's and Jack's eyes staring at her as though she could provide the answer. "Are you saying that this *is* Colette's dress?"

Elizabeth continued to stare at Debbie. When she spoke her voice was void of any emotion. "No. That would be impossible. But somebody did a lot of research and went to a lot of trouble just to perpetrate a practical joke. I want to know why and who." She walked toward the door, signifying that the discussion was over.

Before opening it, Elizabeth stopped and faced Debbie. "I don't want any unfavorable publicity. If someone has something against you--if any further incidents occur, no matter how insignificant--I want to be notified immediately. Is that understood?"

Debbie nodded and reached for her purse, remembering the strange note she had received. She knew she should tell Elizabeth about it, but wouldn't that place her job on the line? It had taken her a long time to get this far. She didn't want to blow it now.

"Is there anything else?" Elizabeth repeated.

"No. I'm sure that this was just someone's idea of a sick joke. It won't happen again." She forced a smile and gracefully walked out.

As she did she heard Elizabeth turn to Jack and say in a voice loud enough to be heard, "Just one more incident and she's gone. Is that understood?"

The statement fueled Debbie's state of confusion. Why had Elizabeth turned against her? She was not to blame for the dress, the note, nor that man stalking her.

Or was she?

Chapter 8

Debbie sunk down on the couch and massaged her forehead. She felt the beginnings of a headache. Maybe if she rested, it might go away. She was just starting to relax when she heard a knock on the door. So much for resting. She sighed. Moving to the door, she called out. When she got no answer, she cautiously opened the door a crack and peered into Annie's anxious face.

"Someone once said that we poison our lives with worry. I don't want that to happen to you, child. I saw you coming here, and by your looks, I thought you might feel like talking."

"Annie, come in." Debbie smiled gratefully. "Thanks for stopping by."

Once they were sitting down, Annie said, "Tell me, child, what's wrong."

Debbie took in a deep breath. "Annie, I think someone--"

Another knock on the door interrupted them. This time it was Jack Armstrong. When Annie saw him, she immediately stood up and headed toward the door. "I'll be back, Miss Gunther, so you can finish explaining how and when you'd like your suite cleaned."

Debbie immediately understood. "That's fine, Annie. Thank you for your concern."

She walked her to the door and gently closed it behind her.

When she turned, she found Jack behind the bar mixing

himself a whiskey sour. "Would you like a drink?"

Debbie shook her head and flopped down on the couch.

"You made a terrible mistake," Jack said. He didn't speak again until he finished fixing his drink. He joined Debbie on the couch. "I'm here, Debbie, to help you. Don't ever make the mistake again of going to Ms. Elizabeth." He took a long swig of his drink before continuing. "After you left, I had a very hard time convincing Ms. Elizabeth to let you stay. She wanted to cancel the show right there and then. She's afraid-- and rightly so--of any bad publicity. She could very easily fire you, and get another impersonator. You realize that?"

Debbie felt like sinking deeper into the couch. "I need this job to open doors for me."

"Then let me help you." He leaned forward so he'd be closer to Debbie. "If you have any more unusual things happen, let me know. Don't go to Ms. Elizabeth--she's got enough to worry about, especially now that her father's dying. She'll have no time to hear your problems.

"I, on the other hand, am here to help. I'll find who sent you that dress and why. Then I'll make sure that he never bothers you again." He stood up. "You have nothing to worry about. In return, all I want from you is that on stage and off stage you become Colette. Act like her, think like her. Become her. Can you do that?"

That sounds too easy, Debbie thought. She nodded.

"Good. Just remember: I'm talking about impersonating Colette twenty-four hours a day. You do this, you get a bonus. Anytime you want a meal from this casino, it's yours free. So is this room. I'm also providing you with five-thousand dollars worth of chips to gamble with downstairs anyway you want. Whatever you win, it's yours to keep. And on top of that, if you give the best Colette performance, I will personally guarantee that Hollywood will be calling."

Debbie stared into Jack's face, trying to study him,

trying to find an alternative motive. "Why are you doing this?"

Jack smiled and finished his drink.

* * *

Debbie had expected a full rehearsal, but instead she found an empty stage. She threw her arms up in desperation and began to walk out.

"Leaving so soon?"

Debbie turned and saw Bill walking toward her. Wild, unharnessed dark hair framed a square face with medium-sized brown eyes. For a second, his eyes held her, almost frightening her. But his coarse looks softened as he smiled. He reached out and wrapped one bulky arm around her shoulder. "Finally, she's here." He held her tight.

"I'm sorry I'm late. I just had some business to take care of. Where's everyone?" She wished he would take his arm off her, but she didn't resist his embrace.

"I don't want a full rehearsal until I hear your ideas. Which number do you plan on doing?"

"Colette always opened with a fast, catchy tune. I thought-"

"Let's go to the showroom where we can sit and talk. We'll be more comfortable, plus we'll be able to view the stage as the audience does." As he led her there, his arm slowly traveled down Debbie's back. His opened palm patted her bottom. Instinctively, Debbie moved away.

"What's wrong?" Bill asked. "I thought you were hired to replace Colette. She was a very friendly person."

"I was hired to impersonate her on the stage."

"And from the way Jack talks, off stage too. So you might as well get used to it, baby." He drew her close to him and forced his lips on hers. She balled her hands into fists and pounded his chest, but his grasp was too strong. She tried pulling away and after a while, he released her.

Her sudden naked rage made her lose all logical thought. "Don't you ever--" Something in his eyes--wild and angry, and filled with venom--made her stop.

"Yes?" The word was whispered through lips tight with suppressed anger.

"I think it'd be best if I come back later." She turned and forced herself to walk at a normal pace. Bill grabbed her arm and swung her around.

His jaw was stiff with anger, and his eyes bored into hers. "While you're gone, listen Miss Prissy, I want you to think about today. I would also like to remind you that I am your director, and if you expect to get anywhere in this world, you must do as I say. I'll be in the Executive Suite until about eight. I'll expect to see you there."

"And if I don't show up?"

"Rehearsal tomorrow is at three. It can be a lot of fun or pure hell. The show can be the best or worst. You choose." He released her arm but not before he brushed his hand past her breast.

* * *

"You son-of-a-bitch," Jack said between clenched teeth. He had waited until Debbie left to approach Bill. "What the hell do you think you're doing?"

Bill stared at him through mocking eyes. "What are you talking about?"

"Cut the bullshit, Bill. If you do anything to ruin my plan concerning Debbie--"

"What the hell should I care about Debbie? She's not Colette." Bill felt anger boil within his veins.

"True, but she's the closest we have."

"The closest *you* have."

Jack exhaled audibly. "I know you loved Colette, and the two of you were going to get married. But this is totally different. I suggested bringing in Debbie for personal reasons which have nothing to do with you."

The pressure built deeper inside Bill, and he felt his lips tremble with anger. "I know why you had Debbie brought in, and I don't like it one bit."

"I don't give a damn whether you like it or not, besides, it's none of your fucking business. All I'm asking is for you to keep your nose out of it and your damn mouth shut."

"And if I don't?"

"Do you really want me to answer that?"

Bill looked away.

Jack took several steps toward Bill so that now he stood very close to him. "Let me just remind you about one thing: you owe me. You ran up a tab with the casino for seven-hundred thousand dollars, and I used my power to make the markers disappear." Jack repeatedly pressed his index finger against Bill's chest. "So don't forget that...buddy, because I won't." Jack looked toward the stage. "You do your job--and let me do mine."

Long after Jack had left, Bill continued to stare at the closed door leading out of the showroom. They were solid, heavy doors made to resemble gold. False gold--just like all of the glitter in Las Vegas was fake. "I swear, you son-of-a-bitch," Bill mumbled to the space Jack had just vacated, "I'll find a way to ruin your plans--even if it means hurting Debbie. What the hell do I care?"

She wasn't, after all, Colette.

Chapter 9

Elizabeth looked stunning in a simple beige two-piece outfit. But it was her companion, Jack, who attracted Debbie's attention. He was wearing a white *gi*--a karate uniform--with a black belt.

When Elizabeth saw Debbie, she waved for her to join them. "Jack's participating in a karate tournament in half an hour. They are fascinating to watch. Why don't you join us?"

Debbie glanced up at the casino's half-chandeliers mounted on mirrors. Their reflections gave her the impression that they were whole. Her eyes drifted back to Ms. Elizabeth. Debbie knew she was expected to attend. But still she ventured to say, "I'm meeting with a reporter at seven."

"We'll be back in plenty of time. It'll only take Jack five minutes to defend his number one position. Someone is always challenging him, but nobody has ever managed to beat him in the last three years."

* * *

It took Jack an hour-and-a-half to defend his title, but in the end, he again walked out with the trophy. Debbie congratulated him and glanced at her watch. In half an hour she was supposed to meet Dan.

At six-fifty-eight Debbie, wearing a simple denim skirt and matching pale blue blouse, stood in front of her closet contemplating her clothes, wondering what to wear. She was about to reach for a soft green evening gown when she heard a knock. "Damn!" she said as she ran to answer it.

Dan looked dashing in his three-piece dinner suit. He seemed a bit surprised when he first saw Debbie, but soon a wide, warm grin covered his face. "Are you going to leave me standing here all night long?"

"No! Of course not." She stepped aside. "Please, come in."

"I take it your meeting with Ms. Elizabeth was satisfactory." When he sat down, he placed his right arm on top of the couch as though he was hugging the cushion.

"Not exactly." Debbie answered, and before she realized what she was doing she had blurted out the entire incident at Elizabeth's office. "The part that terrifies me is that small tear on the dress. How did the practical joker know such a small detail?"

"That's an easy one. All he had to do was be an avid reader." Dan took off his jacket and undid his vest and tie.

"I don't think so." Debbie raised her two index fingers and formed a steeple against her lower lip. "Out of all the stuff that's been written about Colette, how many times have you read about that tear? I never knew about it, at least not until Ms. Elizabeth mentioned it. Yet, evidently it was in the exact same spot. The exact size. It was like this person had seen it, and that frightens me."

"Did Ms. Elizabeth have any theories?"

"No." Debbie shook her head. "But she ordered Jack to find out who sent that dress and why." Fearing that her emotions were threatening to surface, she took a deep breath before continuing, "Dan, she wants to cancel the show if anything else happens."

"Isn't that kind of drastic?"

Debbie shrugged. "Can you help me?"

Dan unbuttoned the first two buttons of his shirt. "How?"

Debbie stared at him. What was he doing?

"What can I do to help?" Dan repeated.

Debbie shook herself out of her startled state and said, "Find out who sent me Colette's dress and why. I think someone is stalking me."

Dan sat perfectly still, his eyes wide-open, his mouth slightly ajar. Slowly, he closed it. "What gives you that idea?"

"There's been a man following me wherever I go. He was with me in California. Now he's here in Las Vegas."

"Do you know who he is?"

"No, I don't."

"Has he made any contact with you?"

"He sent me a note."

Dan cocked his head in alarm.

"It wasn't very threatening," Debbie added. She reached for her purse, dug through it for the note, and handed it to Dan. As he read it, she studied Dan and wondered if maybe she hadn't acted too impulsively. Trying to diminish its importance she said, "It's probably nothing. Someone's idea of a joke. That's all." She forced some cheerfulness into her voice. "Now, if you'll excuse me, I'll go change. One thing this business has taught me is to dress quickly." She started toward the bedroom.

"Don't bother," Dan said, stuffing the note into his shirt pocket. "I'm keeping this so I can get it analyzed. I'll let you know if I find anything out."

Debbie nodded, wondering if that was really wise. "Why shouldn't I change?"

"I'm taking you to a greasy hamburger joint I know that's close to The Meadows."

"The what?"

"It's a shopping mall. And this little joint I'm talking about is just a few blocks away from the mall. Any objections to going there?"

Debbie's mind worked like an automatic ball server, searching for an answer. "I...I promised Jack that I would act like Colette, and she would never set foot in a 'greasy spoon joint.'"

"Do you really think that by going there your career will be over?"

"People are just beginning to accept me as Colette," Debbie said. Her voice sounded defensive.

"I've been told that once you set foot on that stage there is no telling you apart from Colette. But that's only on the stage. Off the stage you're still Debbie Gunther, and that's who I want my story to be about."

Debbie crossed her arms in front of her. "You don't know Debbie. She's not sophisticated at all." *Mouse-like* was the way Grandma had described her the day she kicked Debbie out of the house.

"People shouldn't always be sophisticated, and if Debbie is not sophisticated, then that's perfectly fine with me." Dan smiled as he reached out and held Debbie's arm. "How about it? I want to take Debbie out."

Debbie bit her lip and was only aware of the action when she tasted the warm blood. "We'll give it a try," she said.

"Now you're talking, lady," Dan said as he offered Debbie his arm. "Tonight we're leaving Colette behind and taking Debbie out."

* * *

"Mmmm," Debbie said wiping her mouth. "You're right. These hamburgers and fries sure are greasy, but boy!--are they delicious."

Dan smiled. "I'm glad you like them." They continued to eat and when they finished, he reached for his wallet and left a two dollar tip. "I can't believe that the meal is over, and I haven't even started with the interview. It seems like we've talked about everything, but Debbie Gunther." Dan paid the bill and led Debbie back to his car. "How would you like to walk the Strip?"

"I'd love that."

"I get the feeling that you are avoiding talking about Debbie Gunther," Dan said pulling out of the restaurant's small parking lot. "Why's that?"

Because Debbie's dull.   Unloved, Debbie thought. Without Colette, I'm nothing--just a girl whose father doesn't even want her.

Debbie felt a hand wrap around hers. She turned her head so she could look at Dan. He was staring at her, a puzzled look stamped on his face. The light turned green and someone behind them honked. He withdrew his hand and gripped the steering wheel, then drove off. "Are you all right?" he asked. "You looked like you were miles and miles away."

Debbie numbly nodded. "Yes, of course, I was just thinking."

"About?"

"About how much I want to succeed. How much I have to succeed." By now she could see the Strip alive with its millions of lights.   Huge billboards announced stage acts. Computerized screens showed rolling dice, the winning poker hand, and roulette wheels. Casino names and logos flashed brightly in its multi-colored lights.

Debbie had once heard that the casinos on Las Vegas Blvd. had so many lights that a person could read a book at night. Now she knew why people said that. "Dan, I have a big favor to ask."

"Shoot."

"That stuff that I told you about my life being threatened, please forget it. If Ms. Elizabeth finds out, she'll close the show."

Dan made the face of a pained animal. "Debbie, that's my lead. My readers--"

"*Please*, Dan."

Dan screwed up his face one more time and made a noise like he was clearing his throat. "All right. I'll hold on until after opening night.   Then I'll come up with a story like

'Courageous Star Puts on Show in Spite of Threats.' How's that sound?"

Now it was Debbie's turn to wear the disapproving frown. "I'm not very courageous."

"In that case I'll put one stipulation to holding back the information."

"What's that?"

"If any more unusual things happen, promise me that you'll call me immediately."

Debbie eyed Dan, trying to read his thoughts. "Why?"

For a second Dan looked startled. "Because I want an exclusive on this." Then in a much softer voice he added, "And also because I care." He pulled into the Crystal Palace's parking lot which faced the fountains where life-sized statues of royalty appeared to play in the water. Every hour on the hour, the fountains erupted and fireworks lit up the sky. "Have you seen the fireworks yet?"

Debbie shook her head.

"What about the volcano over at the Mirage? Have you seen it erupt?"

Again Debbie shook her head.

"How about the sinking of the ship at Treasure Island Casino?"

Debbie stared at him.

"Girl, you're in for a treat. Come with me," he said as he opened the car door.

As they walked through the Crystal Palace Casino's perfectly trimmed garden, which represented mankind's triumph over nature, Debbie said, "A little while ago you said that we hadn't talked too much about me. Now it's my turn. What about Dan? What is he like?"

Dan shrugged. "Like a typical reporter, I suppose."

"Why isn't a handsome, young man like you married?"

A painful look covered Dan's face. "I was once. But that was a long time ago." They had now reached Caesar's

Palace and he held her elbow, helping her up the stairs. "Inside that small, round building are several holograms of the inside of Caesar's Palace. You'll see Anthony and Cleopatra-- or maybe it's Julius Caesar and Cleopatra--and several other miniature Roman people dancing and feasting. Then wait until you get to go to Caesar Palace's Mall. It has statues which come to life."

They stepped onto the automatic walkway and inside the palace.

* * *

Debbie felt completely fascinated by the two white tigers on display at the Mirage. "Aren't they just absolutely majestic?" Debbie asked.

But Dan wasn't paying attention to the animals behind the glass wall. Instead, his eyes were glued on a little girl, perhaps no more than five or six years old. She wasn't an exceptionally beautiful girl, but she was cute.

"Do you know her?" Debbie asked.

Dan shook himself, as though coming out of a trance. "Uh, no. I don't think so anyway." Abruptly he reached for Debbie's hand. "Come on. Let's go."

They walked back to the Crystal Palace Casino, Dan urgently leading her back. They did not stop at the Mirage's erupting volcano, nor at the sinking ship at Treasure Island, nor at the dancing water fountains at the Crystal Palace. This time he ignored the garden retreats and instead led Debbie straight to the elevators. "Who was that little girl?" Debbie asked.

"What girl? What are you talking about?"

"Dan, I saw you. You kept staring at that little girl as if you knew her. Who is she?"

Dan shook his head. "She was no one, Debbie. I already told you that." His voice was quiet, his tone sad.

An elevator door swung open and Debbie turned to Dan. "Would you like to come up?"

Dan paused as though considering the offer. Then he sighed, a long-drawn breath from deep inside him. "Thanks, but no." He kissed her forehead. "But keep me in mind if you need someone."

Chapter 10

Debbie opened the door to her suite and was shocked into frozen immobility. Her suite had been filled with roses--dozens and dozens of them. All yellow, with a single red rose in the middle. Debbie remembered reading in Colette's biography that Colette had received similar flowers on the day she died.

The maitre d' had walked onto the stage carrying the bouquet which Colette received with open arms. She reached for the card and read it. "This is absolutely marvelous," she said. "The card is signed 'From one of your fans: Richard Porter.' Is he here tonight?"

Richard Porter turned out to be a teenager who was sitting on the opposite side of the room. With his family's encouragement, he hesitantly stood up and walked to the stage. He turned the color of a ripe apple as Colette kissed him and thanked him for his thoughtfulness. With a plastered smile, similar to that on Mr. Potato Head, the teenager returned to his seat while Colette pulled up a stool and exchanged the flowers for a guitar.

Ten minutes later Colette was dead, and the newspapers labeled that particular arrangement of flowers as the Bouquet of Death.

Now Debbie stood surrounded by at least thirty to forty Bouquets of Death. Feeling like a zombie, she drifted from arrangement to arrangement, searching for the sender's card.

She was beginning to think that there wouldn't be any when her eyes landed on the third bouquet from her right.

There, almost hidden by the leaves, was the tiny envelope.

Debbie ripped it open. The message read:

To Debbie--

because you know the truth about Colette.

It was unsigned.

She stood, staring at the words, their meaning not clear to her. Her eyes drifted toward the open door. She had to talk to Dan.

She thought about Ms. Elizabeth and dashed out of the suite, slamming the door behind her. The deep blue carpet sank beneath Debbie's feet as she hurried to catch the elevator. Once she reached the second floor, she sped past the hissing-noise of the roulette wheel and the small horseshoe blackjack table running down in double rows. She had almost reached the front door when someone stopped her.

"Aren't you Colette?" a wide-eyed fan asked.

"I'm Debbie. I impersonate Colette." She glanced anxiously at the door leading outside.

"That's what I meant. Hey, what about getting a drink? My treat, of course."

"Thanks, that's sound like a marvelous idea." Debbie remembered, in spite of her fear, to smile and to say Colette's favorite word: *marvelous*. Then she quickly added, "But I'm in a hurry."

By the time she reached the parking lot, Dan's car was gone. Debbie stood staring at the multi-colored neon lights that wound down the Las Vegas Strip. Feeling as though she'd been thrown into a bottomless pit with no hope of escape, she made her way back to her suite.

As she walked through the casino, Debbie was almost oblivious to the clattering of the dice and the flashing of silver and blue-backed cards. She noticed several people pointing to her, but she ignored them.

It'd be at least fifteen minutes before she could call Dan. Panic gripped her like an animal caught in a snare. In fifteen minutes a lot could happen. Her stalker might, for instance, walk up to her and... The unfinished thought sent her running back to her suite.

The aroma of the freshly-cut flowers compounded the terror in her. Maybe Dan would be home by now. With panic-filled clumsiness, Debbie opened the phone book, looked up his number, and dialed as fast as her finger would move. The phone rang once, twice, three times...

Please answer.

...four, five...

Please be home.

But the phone only continued to ring. She slammed it down.

She tried sitting by the phone, but she felt so wound up that she found it impossible to remain still. Another ten minutes went by. She was being silly, getting so upset about nothing. What harm was there in receiving flowers? But still...still...

Surely, he's home by now. She misdialed two times before she finally heard the phone ring. She held her breath in anticipation. She was about to hang up when she heard it being picked up. Debbie expected to hear Dan's familiar voice, but instead a woman's deep, throaty voice answered, "Hello?"

Debbie considered hanging up, thinking she'd gotten the wrong number again. But since that would be rude she decided to ask for Dan.

"It's for you, Baby." Her voice was coated with honey-sweetness.

"This is Dan."

In spite of her fear, Debbie felt a pang of jealousy at the faceless woman who had answered the phone. She wanted to scream at Dan, demand to know who she was. But she knew she had no claim on him.

"Who's this?" came Dan's voice over the phone. He

sounded almost upset at being interrupted.

"Dan?"

Silence. Then, "Debbie? Is that you?"

"Dan, I need you. Something awful's happened."

"What happened?"

"I can't say, Dan. Not over the phone. Can you come over?"

A small pause, followed by the muffled sound of a hand being held over the phone while he obviously consulted with Sexy Voice.

"Are you in danger now?"

"I don't know." A nervous glance around the room. "I'm not sure."

"I'll be there."

"Please hurry."

* * *

Dan stood staring wide-eyed at the flowers. "One joke is enough," he said. "Two could mean trouble."

Debbie frowned. She didn't need him to scare her any more.

"Do you have any idea who sent all of these flowers?"

Debbie shook her head.

"No problem. Whoever did it just made his first serious mistake."

Debbie's eyebrows rose in an arch. "What do you mean?"

"That all we have to do is trace the flowers back to the florist and find who put the order in."

"But we don't even know which floral shop sent them. There was a card, but it didn't have the florist's name."

"A card? You didn't tell me. Can I see it?"

Debbie handed it to Dan. He read it, then looked up at her. "What does this mean?" He handed it back to Debbie.

"I'm not sure." She swallowed. "Do you think it's a

death threat? Since I know about Colette, I know that this is a Bouquet of Death. Do you think I'm interpreting this right? Is it a death threat?" She felt her body shake.

"I hope you're wrong, Debbie, but we can't take the chance. We'll assume the worst, and take it from there. What we've got to do is find out who sent these flowers."

"How do we do that? We don't even have the name of the flower shop."

"Somebody had to let the delivery person in. Maybe he noticed the uniform or a hat with a logo or something."

"And if that doesn't work?"

"We'll go to step number two."

"Which is?"

"Going to the flower shops. You've got to realize that this is a unique order. All we have to do is call around until we find the shop which sent them. I'm sure the florist will remember an order like this."

"I hope so." She felt icy tentacles of despair engulf her. "I need a drink. Would you care for something?"

"No. It's kind of late for a drink now."

"All I'm having is orange juice," Debbie said defensively. "Are you sure you don't want any?"

Dan's eyebrows knit slightly. "Orange juice at night? No, thanks. I only touch that stuff early in the morning."

"Does that mean you'll spend the night here?" Her tone was light, but deep inside she was asking a serious question. She didn't want to be alone tonight.

"No. I need to get back to my apartment." From the tone in his voice, he could have been talking about something as unimportant as the weather.

So you can return to Sexy Voice, I bet. "I'm sorry," Debbie said. "I did interrupt your date to bring you all the way over here."

Dan frowned. "Jenny's not a date. She's just a...friend."

A good friend, Debbie added silently. Out loud she said, "I won't keep you. Thanks for coming."

Dan held her eyes as though analyzing her. "Will you be all right?"

Debbie nodded. "I think so. It was stupid of me to carry on like this just because of some silly flowers. Hell, I should feel honored. This must have cost a pretty bundle." Debbie forced a smile. "Yeah, I'll be okay. Maybe we can meet tomorrow and try to figure this out."

He stared at her for a considerably long time. "I'll call," he said.

"You do that," she said, gently closing the door behind Dan.

She leaned on the closed door, staring at the flowers, wondering if they were her death warrant. Then with robot-like movements, she headed toward her bedroom closet, reached for a top box and carefully opened it. She removed the wrapped bundle from its box and pealed away the tissue until she found Poo Bear, her childhood teddy bear.

It stared at her through its one button-eye. It had lost the other eye while still living at Grandma's. "Buttons are expensive. I don't plan to spend my hard earned money on trash like that," Grandma had said.

When Debbie moved in with Daddy, she considered sewing a new button on, but she never did. Daddy didn't love her. If she wasn't worthy of his love, then certainly she wasn't worth the two new buttons it would take to restore Poo Bear's eyesight.

Debbie clasped Poo Bear close to her bosom, desperately seeking the security she longed for.

Chapter 11

Dan had full intentions of heading straight back to his apartment. But instead he found himself in the casino, sitting near the bar surrounded by crystals. Across from him was the dance floor and four couples were doing poor versions of the twist. He sipped his Colorado Bulldog and turned his back on the dancers.

"Hey, Dan."

He glanced toward the sound of the voice. It was Michele Bolds, an ace reporter for a competitive magazine. "Mind if I join you?"

"It's a free country." He drained his Colorado Bulldog.

"Ooooh, are we in a nasty mood?"

Dan turned around and ordered a Love Potion and smirked.

"I heard you got an exclusive on the Colette impersonator--what's her name?"

"Debbie Gunther."

"What's she like?"

Soft. Feminine. Nice. "She's normal." He took a large gulp of his drink. "I guess."

Michele's features softened as she studied Dan. "It's

her again, isn't it?"

"I don't know what you're talking about." He ordered a Pink Lady. He still hadn't finished his Love Potion, but he figured he would by the time his next drink arrived.

"Your wife."

"She's dead."

"I know she's dead--and you've got to stop blaming yourself."

"Why? I killed her." The bartender placed the Pink Lady in front of him. Dan stared at it. He still hadn't finished his Love Potion.

"Dan--"

He held his opened hand up. "Stop. I know what you're going to say. Just spare me the lecture."

Frowning, Michele turned to the bartender and ordered a Bloody Mary. "I just feel you should give us girls a chance."

"Why? So you can end up dead too?"

Michele stepped off the bar stool. "Call me when you stop feeling sorry for yourself." She stormed off without waiting for her drink.

Dan continued to stare at his Pink Lady.

"Shit!" He set a twenty-dollar bill on the bar to cover Michele's Bloody Mary and his own drinks.

He headed back to the elevator, back to Debbie's suite.

* * *

Debbie changed into a bright red teddy with black trimming, brushed her teeth, and laid down. Just as she reached for her book, she heard a knock.

Debbie rolled out of bed, grabbed her short silk robe and without opening the door she asked, "Who is it?"

"It's me, Dan."

Debbie put on the robe and opened the door. "Come in," she said. She noticed the slight smell of alcohol.

She led Dan to the couch. When she sat beside him, the flap on her robe fell open as she crossed her legs. She immediately rearranged the wayward flap. "I'm glad you decided to come back," she said.

"Well, I'm not so sure about that myself," Dan answered.

Debbie leaned back on the couch and as she did, her robe once again fell open. This time she didn't bother to rearrange it. "Then why did you come back?" She noticed that her tone was cool.

Dan's eyes fell on Debbie's exposed upper thigh. He quickly glanced away, wetting his lips. "I feel I owe you an explanation." Again he glanced at her thigh, but this time his eyes remained glued there.

"For what?" Debbie asked.

His eyes moved up to meet hers and remained there for a long time. "Oh, the hell with it," he said as he drew her closer and kissed her. His right hand fell to her exposed thigh and gently stroked it.

Abruptly he stopped. "I'm sorry," he said, pulling away. "This is wrong. I'm so sorry." He stood up and without looking at Debbie, he let himself out, gently closing the door behind him.

* * *

Fatigue invaded Jack's body like thousands of tiny jabbing fingers. He slumped down in the back of the chauffeured Rolls. He was waiting for the arrival of the private jet named *Patty*. It'd be coming in from Dallas. Naturally, it'd have to be late.

Five minutes later, off on the distant horizon Jack spotted the privately-owned jet. He straightened up as he watched it approach. Before the jet landed, Jack ordered the chauffeur to drive onto the parking ramp.

For the convenience of his V.I.P. customers, he had made the proper arrangements with the airport personnel so that his Rolls and limousines could go directly onto the parking ramp instead of inconveniencing his clients by having them go through the terminal.

When Jack spotted Harry stepping out of the jet, he nearly laughed out loud. Harry hadn't changed a bit. He still fit the pattern of the typical Texas millionaire: tall, powerfully built, and somewhere in his fifties. His expression was that of a man who was accustomed to getting his own way. He wore a western suit and expensive cowboy boots with a matching cowboy hat. He sucked on an expensive Havana cigar and carried a light-gray attaché case.

"Harry, it's good to see you." Jack extended his hand in greeting. "Welcome back to Las Vegas."

Harry shook his hand. "It feels damn good to be back." He took off his cowboy hat and wiped his brow as he glanced at the setting sun. "Damn hot."

"You'll find that the Crystal Palace's temperature is perfect." Jack led Harry toward the Rolls. The chauffeur jumped out and held the door open for them.

"Only damn way I'll get used to it is if everything has been set and I won't have a damn thing to worry about."

"Everything is just like you wanted it."

"What about Colette?" Harry asked as he slid into the Rolls. The chauffeur closed the door behind him.

"Her name is Debbie Gunther, and you will swear she is Colette." He signaled to the chauffeur that they were ready to take off.

"Her name is Colette, not Debbie." Harry puffed deeply on his cigar. "And you damn well better remember that."

"Yes, of course." Jack felt as though he should salute this man. "She is Colette."

A tiny frown appeared on Harry's face. "You do understand that nothing is to happen until after opening night."

Jack nodded. "I'm well aware of that fact."

A wide grin covered Harry's face. "That's damn good! In that case, take care of this." He handed Jack his attaché case. "I trust you know what to do with it."

"Of course." Jack nodded agreeably. He didn't need to open the briefcase to know that inside neatly banded stacks of bills awaited him. He had no idea how much he was holding, but once he got into the casino's cage, he'd count it.

He was hoping for something between a quarter of a million to half a million dollars.

* * *

Debbie stared at the alarm clock: three-o-seven--only three-o-seven. The night crept by at a snail's pace. She fluffed up her pillow and closed her eyes.

Less than half-an-hour later, she was wide awake. She got up, poured herself a glass of juice, opened a book, and read.

During the next two-and-a-half hours, she read less than three pages. She had no idea what she had read.

At exactly six in the morning, Debbie called Annie.

* * *

"What in heaven's name is so important that you would have me drag my ass all the way over here at this ungodly hour?" Annie stood outside Debbie's suite, her hair brushed, but definitely not combed. Her face looked older, perhaps because of the lack of make-up.

Debbie opened the door just wide enough for Annie to step in, then immediately slammed it shut behind her.

The sight of the flowers startled Annie, and she took a step backwards. "What the--" She stopped, her mouth wide open, her eyes as round as buttons. She crept toward the flower arrangements. "Why did you do this?" she asked.

"I didn't!" Debbie felt on the verge of tears.

"You mean someone sent them?"

Debbie nodded.

"Who?"

"I don't know."

"This isn't good, child." She shook her head. "This isn't good at all!"

Debbie's mouth felt as if it had been stuffed with cotton. She swallowed hard. "What if Ms. Elizabeth finds out? Annie, you've got to get them out of here, now."

"I hate to blow your bubble, child, but there's nothing that goes on in this casino that Ms. Elizabeth don't know about."

The pressure pounded so hard in Debbie's temples that she knew she was ready to explode. "Annie, there was a strange message attached to the flowers."

"Oh?"

Debbie handed her the card. Annie read it and looked up at Debbie. "Good God, child, what does this mean?"

"I'm not sure, but between that and the dress--"

"The dress?"

"Someone sent me an exact duplicate of the gown Colette wore the night she died."

Annie did not scream, simply because she plastered her hand over her mouth. She started to wobble. Debbie held her and led her to the couch.

"Annie, are you okay? Can I get you something to drink?"

Annie was breathing hard. "Give me a second, child." She fanned herself with her hand. After her breathing became more regular she said, "You're the one!"

"What?"

Annie sprang out of the couch. "Oh my God! It's you."

"What are you talking about, Annie?"

"I'm sorry, child, I can't tell you."

"Annie!"

"You'd never believe me. You'd think I had gone crazy."

Debbie reached out and grabbed Annie by the shoulders. "Annie, what's all of this about?"

"As they say, 'Seeing is believing.' I'll show you." Annie was breathless and she sucked in some air. "I gotta go home and get it if I can find it. I hid it. I never actually thought I'd ever use it."

   "Annie, you're scaring me."

   "That ain't nothing, child. Wait 'till you see it. That's
when you will know what real fear is."

Chapter 12

Less than half-an-hour later, Annie returned. She was carrying a stack of plastic bags and her purse. Debbie eyed the bags suspiciously. "That's it?"

Annie glanced down at the bags. "Oh, no. These are just large plastic bags. For the flowers. You did want me to get rid of them, didn't you?"

Debbie nodded. "Then?"

Annie patted her purse. "It's in here." She opened her purse, retrieved a folded piece of paper, and handed it to Debbie. "Two weeks before Colette died, she gave me this."

Debbie glanced at it.

Annie continued, "When she handed it to me, she says, 'Annie, open this up after I'm dead. You'll know what to do with it.' So I did." She took a step backwards and scratched her chin. "To be truthful, child, I was pretty confused, until now, that is. After talking to you earlier this morning, I knew exactly what Colette was talking about. She wrote this letter specifically for you, Debbie Gunther."

"Me? Annie, she didn't even know me."

"Read it, child, you'll see what I mean. In the meantime, I'll start clearing some of these flowers away."

Hesitantly, Debbie flopped down on the couch. Annie

went through the motions of gathering the flowers, but Debbie could feel Annie's watchful eye.

Debbie took in a deep breath and began to read:
Hi!

You probably know me. My name is Colette, or at least that's what everybody knows me by. That is my stage name. My real name--my true identity--is buried in ancient history and is of no importance.

You're probably wondering why I've decided to write to you. I think you already know why, but in case it isn't obvious to you, I'll explain.

It all began with the "gift" which I have--a "gift" which is really a curse. I've had it ever since I was a little girl. I am psychic. I can see the future, and right now the future I see is very bleak.

I know I will never reach the age of thirty, and that thought is depressing. In spite of all the love the world has for me, I am the Princess in a Glass Cage.

I look at everyone with suspicion. I don't know who I can trust because I know that someone who is close to me plans to kill me. And soon he will succeed.

Oh, God! I'm desperate. I can't turn to the police simply because I have a "feeling." If I turn to the public, they'll say I'm seeking publicity. So I'm turning to the only person I can: you--whoever you are, the person reading this letter.

As you read this, you'll know that I have been murdered so I beg you, please find the person (persons?) responsible. The only hint I can give you is that it was done by someone who was close to me.

Somewhere in my short life I have the clue which evades me for the moment, and hopefully you'll figure it out because maybe you're smarter than I am. So I will tell you what I can about my life.

My whole world right now is filled with people who

really care for me--not Hollywood people, but real people with love. My career is the best that it can be and the future...

Well, what can I say about the future? I have more solid offers than I can afford to accept. I should be on the top of the world for the rest of my life.

Yet, I feel the world crumbling under me. Lately, I've had to take more uppers, then so I can rest, more downers. But they don't work anymore. I'm constantly low. To see me, you wouldn't know it. But on the inside I'm crying. I'm dying--all because of the damn curse which lets me know that someone close to me wants me dead. Why? I don't know. Who? I don't know. I just smell betrayal. And I know I will die.

I have no idea what links you to me. I just know that somehow you know the answer--and worse, the killer knows that too. That's why you must find the person who betrayed me. Find him and expose him. If you don't find him, you will end up as dead as I am.

I want to thank you for helping me out, and I want to wish you the best of luck. Just please, whatever you do, don't let the killer go free. Your life depends on it.

Colette

Debbie dropped the letter. She felt as though she had swallowed broken glass. She looked up at Annie, but didn't say a thing. She simply didn't know what to say.

"So are you going to help Colette?" Annie asked.

Debbie continued to stare at Annie.

"You've got to, you know." When Debbie didn't answer, Annie continued, "I read the letter too, child. I know it sounds-- well, strange."

"Strange?" Debbie bolted out of the couch. "It sounds like something out of the *Twilight Zone*." She waved the letter. "And you expect me to believe it?"

"Believe what you want, child, but just for a second,

listen to me. Hell, child, to be one-hundred percent truthful, I'm not sure Colette wrote you that letter. The only reason I thought so is because of that strange message on the flowers."

"What do you mean?"

"We know Sam Capacini didn't really kill Colette. Someone else did. Right?"

"Annie, you can't say that. Sam Capacini shot Colette in a room full of witnesses."

"True, but why did he do it?"

"God told him to--that's what he said right before he died."

"Those are not his words. He said that the Boss told him to do it."

"Right, right. Then he said that the boss sits up high and judges everyone. It's obvious he was talking about God."

"What if he wasn't?"

"It doesn't matter, Annie. The police--"

"It doesn't matter?" Annie's voice rose to a high shrill. "Of course it matters. Colette is begging for your help, and you're turning your back on her?"

"Annie, I have enough problems of my own. There's a crazy out there who's--"

"Going to kill you if you don't stop him."

Debbie froze and stared at Annie. She opened her mouth to speak, but Annie stopped her.

"You wanted to know what the note meant. I'll tell you what it meant. This man who sent you the flowers and the dress is letting you know what he thinks--no, he *knows*--that you know the truth about Colette. What other truth could he possibly be talking about except for the fact that Sam didn't act alone when he killed Colette?"

"Oh, Annie, that's so far fetched. Why would anyone think I know something about Colette's death when I didn't even know her?"

"You and I know this, but that man out there doesn't.

And as long as he thinks you're a threat to his secret, he will haunt you. Now, have you considered this: maybe you do know something, and if you don't figure out what it is, you might as well forget everything because, child, you're going to end up dead."

Chapter 13

Annie was right, or at least partially right. Debbie should concentrate on finding out who was tormenting her, and, if in so doing, she could find the truth behind Colette's murder, then she would do whatever she could to bring about justice.

However, she doubted that she would be able to shed any light on Colette's death. She just couldn't believe there was any possible connection between her and the dead movie star. How Annie could think that was beyond her.

She shrugged, opened the telephone book, picked up the phone, and dialed the first florist's number. Twenty minutes later, she slammed the receiver down and rubbed her eyes.

She reached for her pen and automatically scratched out the next entry. That made four, and a million left to go, she thought disgustedly. How many flower shops could there be in Las Vegas? Debbie dialed the next number and waited for someone to answer the phone. On the third ring a female voice which sounded like an old woman's or a very young child said, "Anita's Flowers. May I help you?"

Without thinking, Debbie immediately broke into her rehearsed speech. "Yes, ma'am. I hope you can. Yesterday, I ordered some flowers for my boss and I charged them to his VISA card. Now I'm really embarrassed to tell you this, but I gave you the wrong number. I really didn't mean to do this. It's just that my boss closed his account and started a new one. That's perfectly fine with me, except that he forgot to tell me, so when I charged the flowers, I billed them to his old account."

"If you hold for a minute I can pull his records. What is the name?"

Debbie paused for effect. "I feel terrible about this, but I was--well, terribly upset at him and perhaps a little bit drunk. So when I ordered them, I thought it'd be cute if I gave you a false name. And I can't for the life of me, remember what name I gave you."

An uncomfortable silence followed. Then, "I'll check the records. Where were the flowers delivered to?" There was a definite note of irritation in her voice. Must be an old lady, Debbie thought.

Debbie gave her the address. The old lady informed her they had made no such delivery and from here on, she'd advise her to stay sober.

Debbie tried two more flower shops with similar results. On the next try, Debbie was luckier.

"Oh, yes!" the voice said over the phone. "I took that order myself. I remember it 'cuz it was so unusual."

Bingo! Debbie thought. Out loud she said, "Yeah, I bet it was." Then in her most convincing voice she added, "Look, just out of curiosity, what name did I give you?"

Debbie could hear a ruffling of papers. "You said your name was Debbie Gunther."

"Yes, that's who the flowers were delivered to."

"And charged to."

Debbie almost dropped the phone. "Wait! Are you saying that the flowers were charged to Debbie Gunther's account?"

"According to our records, Ms. Gunther used her VISA card to make that charge." The voice sounded almost defensive.

No! That's impossible, Debbie's mind screamed. No

one that I know of has access to my VISA card number. "Is there any possibility of an error? A misunderstanding or something like that?"

"I doubt it. A charge that large has to be verified. Everything checked out all right." There was a slight pause, then the florist continued, "Are you very sure this order was charged to the wrong account?"

"There's only one way to find out. Would you mind giving me the VISA number it was charged to?"

"It's against company rules."

Debbie's frustration increased. "How else can I make sure I gave you the right number?"

There was a small pause as though the florist was considering how to do this. "I know," she said. "You give me the numbers and I'll tell you if they match."

"Just a minute. I'll go get the card." Debbie almost tripped over the couch in her hurry to get her VISA card.

A few seconds later she said into the receiver, "I'm back." She noticed that her hand was shaking. She braced herself and read the numbers.

They were a perfect match.

Chapter 14

Jack's unscheduled rounds always included checking on the progress being made at the baccarat table--the one place where an unlucky night for the casino could mean serious danger to that day's profit margin. That would upset Ms. Elizabeth and Jack didn't want that to happen--at least not while Debbie was here.

After reassuring himself that the casino was ahead by a large margin, Jack visited the Dallas millionaire. "I was wondering if everything is okay. Do you need anything?"

Harry shook his head and offered Jack a drink.

"No, thanks, but you go ahead."

Harry headed for the wet bar and began to prepare himself a Wild Turkey. "There is one minor detail I'd like to talk to you about. I've been here a couple of hours, and I still haven't seen Colette."

Jack sat straight up. "She'll be downstairs, by the baccarat tables. If that's not convenient for you, I'll send you a copy of Colette's schedule, and I'll make sure that she's at your disposal."

"That's good," Harry said as he lit his cigar. "But I don't want her to see me--not yet."

Jack smiled. Harry was just like a little boy with a new toy that he didn't know how to handle. "I remember: not until opening night. Right?"

Harry thrust out his hand with his thumbs up. "Damn right!" he said.

As soon as Jack stepped out of Harry's suite, he ordered a security guard to get a copy of Debbie's schedule and bring it to him immediately. He would then personally hand it over to Harry. In the meantime, he would call Debbie and tell her to be by the baccarat tables for the next hour or so.

* * *

Unable to get hold of Debbie by phone, Dan decided to go to the Crystal Palace Casino. He found her near the baccarat table. He smiled and waved.

Debbie smiled back and wrinkled her nose. "Hi, Dan." She was all Colette.

"Why don't we go grab a Coke somewhere?" Dan suggested.

"I can't. Believe it or not, I'm working. Jack called a little while ago, and he wanted me to be down here as Colette for about an hour."

"Why?"

Debbie shrugged. "Publicity, I suppose. Generate interest in the show." Debbie smiled, winked, and waved at a couple who was staring at her.

"I have a pocket full of quarters. Why don't we feed them to those one-arm bandits over there?" Dan pointed to the row of progressive slot machines.

Debbie nodded. They chose a machine, which when fully fed, accepted two quarters instead of the usual three. They reached for the silver and blue padded stools and sat down. Dan faced the machine, Debbie the casino. "You're an investigative reporter. Aren't you?"

Dan nodded.

"I need your help."

Dan stopped playing the slot machine and turned toward Debbie. "Shoot," he said.

She told him about the flowers being charged to her account.

Dan shut his eyes and slowly exhaled. "Debbie, do you have any idea how the flowers got charged to your account?"

Debbie shook her head.

"Let's try to reason it out. Who has access to your account?"

Debbie shrugged. "No one that I know of."

The lady gambling across from them won a four-hundred dollar jackpot and she screamed. Dan congratulated her and turned his attention back to Debbie. "Someone obviously does."

Debbie nodded. "I know, Dan, and that scares me. How else can he get to me?"

Dan thought for a minute then asked, "Did you lose your purse--even for a second--and then recover it?"

Debbie shook her head.

"Did you make a charge somewhere and maybe the carbon copies weren't destroyed?"

"Not that I know of."

Dan noticed Jack standing across the room, staring at them. Dan turned around and dropped two quarters in the machine. He pulled the handle and watched it spin. He got three oranges and eighteen coins came out. "How about that?" he said. He dropped two more coins in. "Where do you keep your card?"

"In my purse."

Dan continued to gamble. "You travel a lot?"

Debbie nodded.

"What about maids? Who does your room here?"

"Annie." It immediately dawned on Debbie where Dan was leading her. "But you're wrong, Dan. Way wrong. Annie is one of the most trustworthy persons I've ever--"

"I've met Annie. And I agree with you. That doesn't sound like Annie." By now Dan ran out of quarters. He searched his pockets for more coins. "Let's change strategy." He looked through his coins and found two more quarters.

"Let's look for a motive. Who would want to send you all those flowers?" He dropped them in the machine.

"I assume it's the same person who sent me the dress and note."

The wheels displayed a cherry and Dan got his two quarters back. Debbie put her thumb up, signifying success. She asked, "By the way, whatever happened with that note?"

"Nothing much. Too many people handled it to get any clear prints. It was written on plain paper available everywhere."

"How did you manage to get the note checked?"

"A good friend of mine in the Las Vegas Police Department owes me a few favors. We trade back and forth quite often." He dropped the coins in the slot machine but didn't pull the lever. "Sorry I wasn't any help."

"At least you tried," she said.

"I guess. I just wish there had been something." Dan pulled the machine's arm and stopped as the screen video displayed a seven, then another seven, then an orange. "Oh, almost had it," he said. "Have you come up with any theories as to why this guy is doing all this stuff?"

Debbie thought for a minute, then decided to try Annie's theory on him. "Yes, I think he thinks I know something which I don't."

"Back up." Dan emptied his pocket, still searching for a quarter. "What is it that you don't know anything about?"

"I think that the man who is doing all of these things is the same man who ordered Colette's death."

Dan's eyes popped opened, giving him an almost comical look. "You're not making any sense." Dan leaned forward, his full attention focused on Debbie.

"If you remember, shortly after Colette died, there were all sort of rumors floating around including one that claimed that Sam Capacini was the low man in a large conspiracy ring. Whatever happened to that theory? Do you know?"

"Yeah, I remember. All of those yellow journalists put a lot of pressure on the police who then launched a thorough investigation. They found that, yes, Sam Capacini did shoot Colette and that he acted alone. There was no conspiracy." He checked the bin for any quarters. "Why did you bring all of this up?"

Debbie thought of the letter and decided against showing it to Dan. Maybe later she would, but not now. "I guess I'm just being paranoid. Strange things are happening to me, and I'm conjuring up ghosts."

Jack interrupted them. He stood to their left, a wide smile on his face. "Hello, Dan," he said offering his hand. "Any luck with this machine?"

"Nah. I managed to lose a roll of quarters, but that's okay, since I also wrapped up some loose ends on my story." He shook Jack's hand.

"Expensive story." Jack directed his eyes toward Debbie. "What about this gal, eh Dan? Isn't she just Colette's duplicate?"

"Very much so."

"Wait 'till you see her in action. Can't tell the difference. You make sure you mention that in your story."

Dan smiled and nodded.

Jack turned his attention to Debbie. "Col--uh, Debbie, be in my office within half-an-hour. It's urgent that I see you."

Chapter 15

Elizabeth rubbed her eyes before resting her forehead in the palm of her hand. She sighed. "And you're sure that's all there is to it?"

Jack nodded. "There's no doubt in my mind. Debbie ordered those flowers and the dress. Rose Ann, our wardrobe's seamstress, will verify that." Although Ms. Elizabeth's face remained emotionless, Jack could see she felt greatly relieved.

"Why would she do that?"

"Publicity. All of the newspapers would pick up the story instantly: 'Impersonator Stalked by Colette's Nightmares.' That kind of thing."

"I never want to see anything like that in any of the papers." Ms. Elizabeth's mouth was a tight line across her face.

"I will personally talk to Debbie."

"You do that. If--"

Elizabeth was interrupted by the buzz of her intercom. The voice said, "CP 1."

Immediately Jack felt alarmed. Ms. Elizabeth was being paged by her phone code. That could only mean trouble. He watched as Ms. Elizabeth listened to the phone. All color drained from her face as she hung up the phone. She looked up at Jack with unblinking eyes. "It's Daddy. He's had another heart attack."

Jack bolted upright. Her father was the only weakness

Ms. Elizabeth had. "How bad?"

"They don't expect him to make it."

Jack watched her walk out the door leaving him alone in her office. He wondered how this incident would affect his plans.

* * *

"Hi, Jack," Debbie said as she stepped into his office. "What did--"

Jack slammed his opened palms on his desk and stood up. "What the hell do you think you're doing?" He walked around his desk toward Debbie.

She froze in the doorway. "What do you mean?" she asked.

"Meaning that you're supposed to be a Colette representative but there you go trashing her image by going to some stupid 'greasy spoon joint'." The fury in his eyes could have started a blaze. He slammed the door shut.

Debbie answered his anger with venom of her own. "What right do you have to spy on me?"

"What right do I have?" His eyes examined Debbie's face with pure, naked rage. "You, my dear Colette, are the one who doesn't have any rights. Not one damn fucking right! You gave me your word. You said that every action you took, every word you uttered, would be Colette's. Then you turn around and go to a damn trash joint where Colette wouldn't even be caught dead."

"I'm sorry," Debbie said. "I didn't see any harm in going. At the time, I was being Debbie, not Colette. Besides, you did say that I should be nice to Dan."

"I did, so what?" Jack headed back to his desk.

"So he's the one who wanted to go there."

"Big fucking deal. You're supposed to be the charmer. Remember? Change his mind. Or is that too hard to do?"

"I--"

"Look, let me put it to you in as simple terms as I can.

There are hundreds of girls out there who would gladly take your job. If you don't want the twenty-four hour job, I'll find somebody else. Is that clear?"

This job was very important to her. It would further her career by opening other doors. If she let this chance slip by, she might have to go back to her pre-Colette days. She couldn't allow this to happen, yet she wouldn't put up with this bullshit. "If you dump me, someone else would pick me up just as fast."

"Don't count on it. You forget that we're the power people. We'll build the publicity around your replacement so high, you'll sink faster than a drowning rat. You have no choice, Colette." He emphasized the word *Colette*. "It's a twenty-four hour job, or it's no a job at all."

Numbly, Debbie nodded.

Jack sat on the edge of his desk. "Good, now that that's out of the way, I have something else to say. I don't want to see a mention of the flowers or the dress in any of the press." His tone was calmer, but his voice still firm. "There's a limousine waiting for you by the main door."

"Where am I going?"

He eyed her strangely. "To the hospital, of course."

"Why?"

"Didn't Bill tell you?"

Debbie shook her head.

"Damn it. He may be a good director, but he sure is an asshole." He frowned. "We have a very valuable customer. Her name is Mrs. Neal and her daughter is sick. Nothing really major, but she is in the hospital. Anyway, the kid loves Colette. Mrs. Neal called and explained the circumstances. Seeing how Mrs. Neal comes in every month and drops several thousand dollars each time, we figured you could spend some time with the kid." He walked over to the door and reached for the knob. "Now, don't forget that you're going as Colette. As of now, Debbie Gunther is dead."

* * *

Someone stood outside the Crystal Palace Casino intently watching as Debbie stepped into the limousine. He had immediately recognized her. But then again he would have, even if she was wearing a disguise. He was tempted to approach her, but he stopped himself, realizing that this wasn't the right time.

After all, he already had a ticket for her opening night performance. He'd slip the maitre d' a fifty dollar bill and request a front seat where she'd be able to see him. He'd love to see the look on her face when she saw him there, sitting out in the audience. It might even ruin her performance. And wouldn't that be wonderful? He'd love it if the entire audience laughed at her. Why, he'd be laughing the hardest.

Then again, he might request a table at the very back, where the shadows would protect him. He wasn't quite ready to face her...yet. He would, he knew, one day soon, but he'd have to wait for the perfect time. In the meantime, he'd be there on her opening night.

Chapter 16

The elevator doors to the Children's Ward opened and Debbie stepped out. She saw a worn-out looking woman in faded jeans and baggy T-shirt heading toward her. "I know you're the one who does Colette, but I'm sorry, I really can't think of your name at the moment."

"That's okay. I'm used to it. It happens quite often. I'm Debbie Gunther." They shook hands. "How's Cindy?"

"Under the circumstances, she's fine." They walked down to the waiting room. "I appreciate what you're doing for my daughter."

"It's my pleasure. I'm glad to help."

"I'm sorry you came here so early. I called you at the Crystal Palace, but you had already left. They decided to run some tests on her. It'll be at least an hour before you can see her. I'm so sorry."

"No problem," Debbie said. "I wanted to bring her something, but I haven't had the chance to buy anything. This will give me time to do so."

"That's not necessary."

"I know, but I want to do it. I'll be back in an hour."

Debbie got back on the elevator. She hoped that the hospital's gift shop would have an appropriate gift, as there were no stores nearby.

As soon as she entered the small store, she spotted Elizabeth standing by the flower arrangement display. She stood with her head hanging low, a perfect picture of defeat. "Ms. Elizabeth," Debbie said softly.

Startled, she looked up. Her face was pale and eyes hollow. "Debbie! What are you doing here?"

"There's a little girl here who requested to see me."

Elizabeth nodded.

"Are you all right?" Debbie asked.

"It's my dad. He's upstairs, dying, and I'm down here looking for a flower arrangement to take to him." She smirked at the irony of the situation. "I'm sorry. Dad always said that weakness is our greatest enemy, but right now I don't feel very strong."

"Is there anything I can do?"

"As a matter of fact, yes. Come upstairs with me. My dad loved Colette. His face would light up whenever he saw her. Lately, he hasn't remembered that she's dead. He keeps asking for her. It would make him so happy. You won't have to stay long. Just say hi, how are you--that type of thing. What do you say?"

She patted Ms. Elizabeth on the back and nodded. "Just let me pick up something for little Cindy first."

* * *

Stuart Lovingsworth turned out to be a skeleton of a man. His cheeks were sunken, and his hair was solid white. It was hard for Debbie to accept the fact that this was the same man who was supposed to be the most powerful man in the casino. Immediately Debbie realized that Elizabeth was the real power behind the Lovingsworth name.

Stuart lay in bed, his chest rising and dropping with each strained breath he took. He had five telemetry leads taped to his chest. Behind him an electro-cardiograph was recording the irregular beating of his heart.

"Daddy?" Elizabeth's voice sounded weak and mousy. She cleared her throat. "Daddy?" This time it was louder, clearer.

Slowly, the old man opened his eyes, and Debbie felt a pang of jealousy when she read the love he had in his eyes for his daughter. She thought of her own father. She had wanted his love so much that she had created what she called her Imagination Daddy.

Debbie had kept a picture of her parents under her mattress, and whenever she wanted to talk to her Imagination Daddy, she retrieved the picture which showed her mother smiling, and a young man--her father--with his arm around her. He was looking at his wife as though she were a fragile flower. Debbie had known that once she was reunited with her father, he would look at her that way too. Instead, he had hated her.

Debbie shook the memory away as she heard Mr. Lovingsworth speak, "Lizzy, honey." His eyes traveled past Elizabeth and toward her. "Colette! How nice of you to come. You two always did travel together. I've missed you, Colette. Why hadn't you come before now?"

Debbie and Elizabeth both exchanged looks but neither of them corrected him. "I'm here now," Debbie said.

"Come, both of you, sit by my side." He barely raised his hand, motioning for them to join him. "I have a story to tell you." His voice was barely above a whisper, and he had to strain to talk.

Elizabeth held his hand and patted it. "Shh. Don't talk now. Save your strength."

"Listen! There's no...later." The old man gasped for air.

Elizabeth's face pinched in alarm. Debbie placed her hand on Elizabeth's shoulder, hoping to reassure her.

For a second Stuart lay still until his breathing returned to as normal as possible. His eyes focused on Ms. Elizabeth's. "Lizzy, you knew that your mother and I didn't get along. I thought of leaving her, but I couldn't. It would've hurt you, and I'd never do that to you. You were seven then and my pride and joy. I wanted to make sure you'd never be hurt. I swore that I would always protect you at all costs."

In spite of her gallant efforts, Elizabeth's eyes watered.

"Remember that, Lizzy, I would never hurt you." He spoke with the urgency of a man who knew his life star was diminishing. "Do you understand?"

Elizabeth nodded.

"There was another woman I loved." Even death could not shroud the beam in his face. His eyes smiled, and his lips slightly curled upwards at her remembrance. "She was twenty-five years younger than me, and her parents were very strict. Her father would have beaten her if he'd known about me." Stuart coughed.

Debbie felt Elizabeth's body stiffen, and she patted her shoulder. Elizabeth glanced at her, her eyes wild as though begging her father not to continue.

"Do you want me to wait outside?" Debbie whispered in Elizabeth's ear.

Elizabeth shook her head and returned her attention to her father. She gasped when she saw the tears in her father's eyes.

"We had a daughter, Lizzy. You have a sister." His eyes squinted, the brows knitted together, and lines between the eyes pulled into a little frown.

For a moment Debbie thought the old man was finished. She glanced at Elizabeth. If she wasn't holding her, if she couldn't feel her tremble, Debbie would have sworn that the news had not affected Elizabeth. She sat still as a statue, stroking her father's hand.

"I knew she had gone into labor. I even knew which hospital she was in. But I couldn't bring myself to visit her. I had so much to lose. It was easier to pretend she never existed." He spoke without pausing, more of a monologue than a dialogue. "Then it was too late. She took the baby and went away. I didn't want her followed. I didn't want to know anything about them." A tear streamed down his cheek and rolled onto the pillow. "I'm dying, Lizzy. Make things right for me so I can die in peace."

"How?" Elizabeth's voice was toneless.

"Find your sister!" Stuart attempted to get up, but all he managed to do was raise his head. "You've got to find her. Please. Do it for me."

Elizabeth frowned.

Stuart lay back down and sighed. "There's more. But please, Lizzy, don't be hurt. I would never want to hurt you-- especially now." He spoke rapidly, as if he knew he had to get it all out before it was too late. "Six years ago, when I first found out I had a weak heart, I made out a new will. Your sister..." He paused for some air. "She's to get..." Again, he paused, as though searching his daughter's eyes for some form of understanding. "She'll get...forty percent of the casino's profit. If you don't find her in six months, then eighty percent of the money is to go to charity."

Involuntarily, Elizabeth dropped her father's hand as though she had been burned.

His trembling arm reached out for his daughter. "Lizzy, please. I have to do this to make up for the wrong I've done her. Allow your old man to die in peace." He seemed to recognize the hurt in Elizabeth's eyes, for he quickly added, "You run the casino. You make all the decisions. It's in the will. All she gets is some of the money." Still seeing no sign of mercy, he grasped his daughter's arm. "Lizzy, please."

His eyes searched Debbie's face and pleaded with her. "Help me, Colette. You were always good in persuading Lizzy."

"Ms. Elizabeth," Debbie said not quite sure what would follow.

Elizabeth glanced at her with the unmistakable gaze of a judge who was about to pass a harsh sentence. Debbie felt herself recoil and was glad that Elizabeth returned her attention to her father when he once again began to speak.

"Don't let me die like this. I just want to do what's right

for both of you." He squeezed as hard as he could. "Please."

"Where is she?" Elizabeth spoke slowly, deliberately. "Who is she?"

Stuart Lovingsworth smiled and released his daughter's arm. "You won't let me down. I knew you'd understand." He leaned back on his pillow and folded his arms in front of him. For a second the only sound in the room was that of the electrocardiograph marking each of Stuart's fading heartbeats. "I don't know where my daughter is. I don't even know what she looks like. I deliberately lost all contact with her mother. Later--much later--I learned that she was dirt poor, but with all my millions, I still turned my back on her. Now it's up to you to help her for me. Find your sister and give her what is rightly hers." Stuart gasped for breath. "Promise me you'll do that."

Elizabeth nodded. "How can I find her? I need something to go by."

Stuart opened his mouth, but nothing came out. The electrocardiograph beeped one last time, followed by its continuous humming. Elizabeth jumped at the sound. "D--da--daddy?"

No answer.

Only the continuous humming.

Debbie stood perfectly still. She could feel the anguish, the hollowness, the vast void Elizabeth was experiencing. She watched as Elizabeth bent over and kissed his forehead. "Good-bye, Daddy," she said, and with detached calmness she looked at Debbie and said, "You'd better call a doctor."

Debbie nodded and turned to leave but by then two nurses were running toward Stuart. Behind them, a doctor followed. Debbie quietly let herself out and headed toward the elevator. She pushed the button for the third floor, the children's ward.

Chapter 17

A casino employee, a young and pretty lady with short-cropped hair, saw Debbie enter the casino. She ran back to her station, picked up an envelope and ran after Debbie. "You have a message." She handed Debbie the envelope.

Debbie glanced down at it and noticed that her name was printed in plain block letters. The writing was similar to that first note she'd received the day she arrived.

"Anything wrong, Miss Gunther?" the runner asked.

Debbie looked up and smiled in spite of the panic which began to gnaw at her. "No, of course not." She tipped the runner a dollar and waited until she had left before ripping the message open. She read:

Debbie,

I heard about Mr. Lovingsworth, so I'm postponing rehearsal. I'll call you later.

Bill

"It's just a note from Bill," she said to herself. "Just a note." She shoved it into her purse.

She didn't savor the idea of being alone in her suite. She glanced at the row of video poker machines. She had barely opened her purse when she heard someone say, "Excuse me, you're Colette. Aren't you?" Debbie turned to face a stout, matronly-looking woman. "I'm Debbie Gunther and on stage I impersonate Colette."

"I knew it!" the woman answered. "Would you mind posing for a picture with us?" She pointed to her right. "That's my husband over there. The one with the camera."

A balding man with thick glasses waved at them. He was smiling.

"Of course," Debbie said, and she smiled back, "but we'll have to step outside. It's against casino rules to take pictures inside."

She led them to the water fountain where they took two sets of pictures: one with him and one with her. They handed her their motel room bill. Debbie turned it over and signed her name.

As she handed it back to the couple, she caught a glimpse of someone dashing away from her view. Remembering to wrinkle her nose and smile, she stared at all the people who had gathered around her.

Somewhere among them, Debbie could feel hate emanating like a blast from the sun. She was studying each of their eyes when she heard Colette's name being called.

She turned and spotted three teenage girls, the giggly type. "Can I have your autograph?" one of the girls--the tall, slim one--asked.

"My pleasure," Debbie said, walking toward them. Footsteps followed her. She stopped and turned. People. People all over. She should be safe. But she didn't feel safe.

Debbie forced a smile and resumed her walk. The girl handed her a piece of paper and Debbie signed it.

"Do you always answer to Colette?" another of the girls asked. Before Debbie could answer, the girl continued, "Is that because you think you're Colette. Do you think you're just like her?"

"No, I don't think I am Colette--"

"Colette!" Someone from behind her called. "Look this way. Hey, Colette!"

Debbie heard him, but ignored him. Maybe the teenager was right. She shouldn't answer to Colette.

"Hey! What's the matter? Think you're too good for us little people?"

Debbie frowned. There was no winning. She turned around to explain. That's when she saw him again: a figure dashing behind a bulky solid marble column.

She turned and ran the opposite direction.

"Hey! What's the matter, sweetheart? The truth hurt?" the same rude man asked, probably thinking she was fleeing from him. He burst out laughing.

Debbie ignored him and continued at a fast pace, her shoes urgently whispering on the sidewalk. She kept her eyes glued to the ground.

In her desperate attempt to outrun her pursuer, she failed to notice the man directly in front of her. He stood with his hands on his hips, his legs slightly spread apart. She looked up at him and held her breath in anticipation.

"Well, I'll be damned," he said. "If it isn't Colette."

Debbie stepped back, but she kept her eyes glued to his face. She had never seen such a big man, but his size could only be a handicap. Surely, she'd be able to out run him.

Even though she was only a foot away from him, he made no efforts to grab her. This, however, gave her little comfort. Her mind screamed and she could feel her heart jammed in her throat.

"You are Colette," the giant repeated. "Aren't you?"

She nodded.

"I didn't scare you, did I?

Still on guard, Debbie shook her head and managed a weak smile. "I was just lost in thought."

"Good, 'cuz it--"

BOOM!

A loud, sudden explosion close to Debbie's feet sent Debbie's heart racing.

The explosion was immediately followed by a second. And a third.

Debbie screamed and simultaneously jumped. She felt like a puppet whose string had been pulled all at once. In her haste to escape, Debbie lost her balance and landed on her buttocks. Her upper torso jerked backwards, and she bumped her head against one of the casino's decorative pillars.

Blinding lights exploded in her brain. Her hands reached for her aching head.

"Miss, are you all right?" the giant asked. He was kneeling by her side and a small crowd had gathered to watch.

Numbly, Debbie nodded. "What--"

"Firecrackers, ma'am." He opened his hand to reveal three used firecrackers. "Someone's idea of a sick joke." With a disgusted look he cast them aside. "Are you sure you're okay? Is there anything I can do? I can take you home or call an ambulance or the police."

Debbie reached for her purse, opened it and retrieved two tickets. "Will you be in town this Sunday?"

"I live here, ma'am."

"Good. That means you can come to my performance--as my guest."

His eyebrows arched and his mouth opened slightly. "You mean that?"

Debbie nodded and handed him the tickets. He put them in his shirt pocket and helped her up. Once she stood up, the pain in her legs and bottom registered in her brain. She ignored it.

"The least I can do is escort you to your car."

"I'm walking," she said. She felt dizzy from the bump on her head. For a few seconds everything spun around, and she closed her eyes. When she opened them, the images slowly reformed into one.

"Then I'll walk with you and make sure nobody decides to play another prank on you." He led her by her arm. "You'd be surprised how many people are afraid of me just 'cuz I'm so big."

Debbie smiled. No, she wouldn't be surprised at all.

Chapter 18

As soon as Debbie reached her suite, she dialed Dan's number from memory. On the fourth ring someone picked up the phone. "Hello?" Sexy Voice again. Damn! Debbie considered hanging up, then decided against it. "May I please speak to Dan?"

There was a small hesitation followed by, "Yeah, I guess."

Dan picked up the phone and listened to Debbie's brief story. He promised to get to her suite as soon as possible.

* * *

"I want to go to the police, Dan. Will you come with me?" Debbie asked. They were sitting on the couch, their legs almost touching. In spite of her fear, Debbie felt a tingling sensation inside her. If only Sexy Voice wasn't around...

"Going to the police isn't a very good idea," Dan answered. He turned toward Debbie and in so doing, their legs touched.

Debbie was very aware of Dan's almost imperceptible movement. She did not move herself over, so that their legs continued to rub against one another. "Why not?" she asked.

Dan put his arm on top of the sofa's back, behind Debbie. "Let's look at it from the police's point of view," he said.

"Go on."

"What can you tell them?"

Debbie felt her body defensively tense up. "Well, there's the firecrackers."

"Kids playing. They weren't even directed at you. You were just in the right place at the wrong time."

Debbie shrugged. "There's the flowers."

"Which you sent yourself."

"I didn't, Dan. I swear, I didn't!"

"Debbie, this isn't me talking." He moved his arm down. It was now resting on Debbie's shoulder. "I'm saying the things the police will probably say."

Debbie's lips were dry, and she wet them. "What about the dress?"

"You placed the order yourself."

"What?"

"I checked, Debbie. The casino's seamstress said that a lady called asking that Colette's red dress be duplicated."

"Dan, that wasn't me."

"She said you placed the call, but of course, she can't swear it was actually you since she's never met you. All she knows is that a lady claiming to be Debbie Gunther placed the order."

Debbie felt all hope drain out, but still she refused to give up. "I have...something else," she said slowly.

"The letter? You could have sent yourself that as well."

"No, I have another letter. One Colette wrote to me before she died."

It was now Dan's turn to be surprised. He stared at Debbie with wide open eyes. "What?"

Debbie proceeded to tell him about how she had received Colette's letter and how Annie suspected that Colette had been murdered by someone other than Sam Capacini. "Sam pulled the trigger," Debbie said, "but, according to Annie, someone hired him to do it. And, the more I think about it, the more I'm inclined to believe it."

"Why?"

"Because of all of this stuff which is happening to me. Annie feels that for some odd reason that same person who ordered Colette's death is now after me."

"Did she tell you why?"

"He thinks I know who he is, or I can figure it out, but believe me, Dan, I've racked my brain trying to come up with a face, a name." She shrugged. "Nothing. Zilch. Zero."

Sometime during her narrative--Debbie wasn't sure when--she had stood up and began to pace the room. Now she stood directly in front of Dan, staring at him; her arms crossed in front of her.

"Can I see this letter?" Dan asked.

Debbie nodded and headed toward the bedroom. A few seconds later she returned, clutching the paper. She handed it to Dan.

His eyes narrowed as he read it. "Are you sure Colette wrote this?"

"I suppose so. Annie said she did."

"That could have been where all those rumors got started."

"What rumors?"

"Remember? About there being more than one man involved in Colette's murder?"

Debbie nodded.

"When Colette died, I did a lot of research trying to find some truth to these rumors. Do you know what I found? Absolutely nothing. Everything pointed to Sam Capacini being the sole killer. Now this letter surfaces, but there's nothing tangible there. It's hard for me to accept it, just like that." He stood up, closely facing Debbie. "But I do believe that something is going on, and I'll help you find out what it is." He reached out and gently stroked her hair.

Debbie stepped away from him just far enough to be able to stare into his eyes. They locked and as though they were moving in slow motion, Dan's head tilted forward seemingly ready to kiss her.

Abruptly, he stopped as though he had changed his mind. Instead, he brushed the tip of her nose with his index finger. "Let's re-read this together. Maybe we can come up with some kind of evidence that we can take to the police." He pulled away from her, breaking whatever spell had been cast on them. "Okay?"

Debbie's heart sank, but she nodded. She walked over to the desk, retrieved a long yellow pad of paper, and handed it to Dan. "In case we want to take notes," she said in answer to Dan's unasked question.

He nodded and began to re-read the note.

Silently, Debbie cursed Sexy Voice.

Chapter 19

Annie was about ready to head home when Carolyn Morales, Ms. Elizabeth's secretary, stopped her. "Annie, you have got to go make your report to Ms. Elizabeth. She's upset because it's way overdue."

"Yes, I know, I know. I've been a trying to get over there, but I've a been so busy. I promise: first thing tomorrow morning."

"No, Annie. Don't wait until tomorrow. Go now. She's in her office."

"She's here? Now? Didn't she take any time off because of her father's death?"

"You know Ms. Elizabeth. She told me she was coming in for an hour or so just to get away from the pressures of the funeral."

Annie nodded, headed to Ms. Elizabeth's office and knocked on the door.

"Come in," Annie heard Ms. Elizabeth say.

When Annie stepped inside she saw that Ms. Elizabeth's eyes were focused on the vast casino lights that maintained their vigilance over the Strip. From somewhere deep inside her, a sob shook Ms. Elizabeth's body. Slowly, Ms. Elizabeth's eyes traveled toward Annie. "Isn't it rather late to be doing your work?"

"I'm all through with my job, Ma'am. I just felt that I should stop by to tell you how sorry I am."

Ms. Elizabeth nodded as an acknowledgment. "Thank you, Annie." Her eyes returned to the lights. "Have you anything else to say?"

Annie hesitated only for a second, and in a loud, clear voice she said, "Debbie ordered those flowers and that dress herself."

"Why?" Ms. Elizabeth's eyes remained glued to the lights.

"She has this silly notion that Sam Capacini was coaxed into killing Colette. Debbie feels that she owes it to Colette to find the person who ordered the killing."

Ms. Elizabeth's eyes drifted toward Annie. Her eyes were cold and hard. "Where would she get an idea like that?"

Annie shrugged. "Who knows? She's a strange one."

"I need to know more. I will not allow Debbie--or anyone else--to taint the casino's reputation." Ms. Elizabeth's jaw stiffened as her eyes bore into Annie. "This Colette thing could only harm the casino." This time her voice contained a forced calmness. "I want her to drop this foolishness immediately, or she can find herself a new job. I'll tell her myself tomorrow."

"Oh, no, no, please don't. She'll listen to me. I'll talk to her."

"See that you do. And as soon as you do I want to know her answer--immediately. Is that clear?" She looked back to the window, signifying the conversation was over.

"Yes, Ma'am," Annie said as she closed the door behind her.

* * *

The ringing of the phone startled Debbie out of a peaceful night's rest. She stared at the alarm clock, then at the transparent crystal phone. It wasn't supposed to ring at three in the morning. She picked up the receiver. "Yes?"

"How did you like my little demonstration, Debbie?"

That voice! Muffled, obviously disguised. Perhaps a handkerchief over the receiver. But in spite of this, it was still familiar. So familiar.

"Did you hear me, Debbie?" the male voice continued. "This time they were firecrackers. Next time, who knows?"

Hang up! Debbie's mind ordered. Hang up! Her body did not obey the simple command. She held the phone to her ear, afraid to let if go. Afraid not to let it go.

"There will be a next time. You know that. Don't you? The firecrackers were just to show you how easy it is to get to you." There was a short pause. "Are you still there?" Another pause, then he continued without waiting for an answer. "Yes, of course, you're still there. You can't hang up because you want to be punished--punished because of what you've done."

Debbie dropped the phone as though it had burned her hand.

Chapter 20

Sweat and fatigue engulfed every inch of Debbie's body. Yet, she felt radiantly alive, for today, more than ever, she put her entire being into her song and dance routine. She knew she was good. She could see it in the stage hands' faces. They stood mesmerized by her charisma. When she finished her performance, they clapped loudly and whistled.

Instinctively, Debbie turned to smile for them, but when she did, her eyes swept past the stage hands to the solitary figure behind them: Dan. He stood leaning against an opened door prop, his face beaming like a lighthouse. "Beautiful." He mouthed the word.

Pride engulfed Debbie, and she swore that her next performance would be twice as good. She winked at Dan, wrinkled her nose, and turned her attention to the director, Bill Davis.

"That was tremendous," Bill said. "I don't know how you do it, but I swear that you're even better than Colette." He put his arm around her and gently squeezed. In so doing, he brought his mouth right next to Debbie's ear. "You stood me up, you bitch," he hissed.

Without giving her a chance to respond, he dropped his

arm and walked away. "You're through for the day, Debbie, but do look me up. There were several things we need to discuss." He turned toward the Crystalites, the casino dancers. "You were all out of sync. You need to do it all over again." He clapped his hands together. "Come on, come on, come on. Time's a wasting. And time is money."

The dancers scurried into their dance positions as Debbie headed toward Dan. "Dan! What are you doing here?" she asked.

"Haven't you heard?" he answered. "Ms. Elizabeth found her sister and my editor, Pete, sent me over to do a small feature on it." He reached for Debbie's hand and wrapped his hands around hers.

"Ms. Elizabeth found her sister? How wonderful!"

Dan nodded. "I agree, and since I was here, I decided to drop by. Do you mind?"

Debbie shook her head and felt herself blush.

Dan smiled, "Actually, I wanted to talk to you about Colette's letter."

"Oh?"

Dan looked around, leaned closer to Debbie and whispered. "Can we go talk some place?"

Debbie glanced at the Crystalites. "I'd really like to watch them so I can see how they fit into the routine. Could we go down there?" She pointed to the showroom. "We can talk and at the same time I'll be able to watch the Crystalites from the audience's point of view."

"Of course," Dan said as he led her down the stairs and toward the center of the showroom. They sat in a booth facing the stage.

"So what was it that you wanted to tell me?" Temporarily, Debbie had forgotten about the Crystalites and devoted her full attention to Dan.

"I've re-read the entire police reports and my own notes- -as well as anyone else's notes I could get hold of. I searched for even the slightest clue that someone ordered Colette's death."

"And?"

"Nothing, not even a small suggestion."

Debbie watched the Crystalites for a few seconds, then returned her attention to Dan. "Colette used drugs."

"I know she did."

"Couldn't drugs be the reason?"

"I doubt it. She was a user--and a discreet user at that. No reason to do her in."

"But they could have."

Dan nodded. "Yes, they could have. Drugs often...lead to murder." He paused and went pale.

"Dan, what's wrong?" Debbie reached for Dan's hands and squeezed them.

"Sorry. It's a long story. Maybe later." He looked up at Debbie through blank, dull eyes. he noticed Debbie's frown, and he gently rubbed it, attempting to massage it away. "Five years ago, I--" He sighed and shook himself. "I'm sorry, I thought I could, but I can't at least not right now."

Picking up the hint, Debbie decided to change the subject. "What did Ms. Elizabeth say about her sister?"

"She was delighted to find her. Ever since word got around that her father was critically ill, many of his silent partners began arriving from New York, Chicago, and Los Angeles. They purchased points into the Crystal Palace Hotel from the Nevada Gaming Commission. For each point that was purchased, Ms. Elizabeth lost some power. She feels that with her sister arriving, this will put a stop to the purchases."

One of the dancers missed a beat, and Bill stopped them all. He yelled at Cindy, the dancer, and embarrassed her by making her do a solo. When Bill turned around, Cindy made a face at him and Debbie smiled, then turned serious. "Dan, something else happened."

"Tell me about it."

"Not here," Debbie said.

"How long until you're free?"

Debbie shrugged. "I'm through for the day, but I'd like to stay here and watch the dancers. Maybe for an hour or so."

"In that case, I'll pick you up in two hours. We're going on a picnic."

Chapter 21

"So tell me what you couldn't tell me at the casino," Dan said. They were sitting on the shore of Lake Mead. A picnic basket lay opened between them. About thirty feet to the right, an elderly man was fishing, and a few feet further, a young boy, perhaps his grandson, was hooking a worm. Except for the four of them, the beach was deserted.

Debbie glanced out into the placid water, feeling peaceful and calm. "Remember the firecracker incident? We didn't know if it had been some kids playing a prank or if someone deliberately threw them at me."

"Uh huh." Dan reached for his fishing gear and began to prepare his rod.

"They were intended to scare me."

"What makes you think that?"

"Last night some man called just to let me know how easily accessible I am. He said the firecrackers were just a warning."

Dan's hand, holding a number-ten hook, froze on its way to the rod. He turned his head to gape at Debbie through wide-open eyes. "Are you serious?" he managed to ask after a pause.

Debbie nodded, "Not only that, Dan, but I've had this really creepy feeling that I'm being followed and constantly watched. At first I thought I was being paranoid, but after the firecracker incident and phone call..." Debbie let her voice fade away.

Dan sat perfectly still, his fishing gear forgotten by his side. When he spoke, it was slowly as though carefully choosing his words. "Did you recognize the voice? Was there anything distinctive about it?"

"It sounded vaguely familiar. I felt it was someone I know--or should know. But the voice was disguised, and I couldn't quite place it." She pulled her legs up against her chest and wrapped her arms around her knees.

"Any idea who it could be?"

Without hesitating she said, "Bill Davis."

"Your director? Why?"

"I got a note from him, and I swear, Dan, the handwriting on the envelope is identical to the handwriting on that first note I got."

"That envelope. Do you still have it?"

Debbie nodded. She looked at the water. It was tranquil, like a pane of glass.

"Can I see it? I have a friend who is an expert on handwriting. He'll be able to--" He noticed Debbie's tears streaming down her cheek. "Debbie?"

"Dan, he tried to put the make on me."

Dan's lips tightened and his chin hardened. "Go on."

"He tried to touch me and forcefully kissed me. Then he threatened me with the show if I didn't sleep with him."

"Have you?"

"No! Of course not." *How could he ask that?*

"And you think that because you turned him down he's after you?"

"Maybe."

"How is all of this connected to Colette?"

"Annie told me that he and Colette were engaged. Maybe she changed her mind and he killed her. And maybe, in his mind, I am Colette. Maybe he's just crazy. I know he gives me the creeps."

"All of these are just speculations, but until we know for sure, I don't want you near him. Is that clear?"

Debbie nodded and suddenly felt like a little girl again, lost and confused. Impulsively, Debbie threw her arms around Dan, her face close to his, inviting him to kiss her. When he kissed her, his mouth was opened wide, his tongue urgently searching hers. His kiss was powerful and consuming, his hug strong. She could feel his need, and she was willing to satisfy him.

What Debbie wasn't expecting was for Dan to pull away. He stood up and walked away from her.

"Dan?" Why had he pulled away? She stood up and began to follow him. "What's wrong, Dan?"

Debbie almost caught up with him. Why did he have to walk so damn fast? "Have I done something wrong?" Debbie felt like a high school girl facing the man of her dreams for the first time. "Dan, please stop." What was wrong with him anyway? "Please."

For a second, Dan slightly hesitated then resumed with his fast pace.

Debbie's confusion gave birth to anger. "Good-bye, Dan. I'm leaving." She headed back toward the blanket they had spread out for the picnic.

* * *

Less than one-hundred feet from them a row of oleanders separated the beach area from a campground. Using the bushes for protection, a man stood watching Debbie.

He had followed her from the casino. In fact, he had followed her all the way to Las Vegas. He had assumed he would wait until opening night, but now he wasn't so sure.

He didn't know why Dan and Debbie were having problems. And he didn't care to find out. All he knew was that Dan was walking away from Debbie, leaving her alone.

He liked that. All of this time, he'd been waiting for the right moment.

Maybe this was it.

He stepped away from the bushes, knowing the shadows would still provide him with ample protection. Now, if he could just lure her away from the open space. Bring her to where he was. Then he would--

He smiled, savoring the thought.

* * *

Dan stood staring at the waters of Lake Mead and shook his head. All of a sudden his life had become so complicated. He sighed. "Debbie, wait!" He ran to catch up with her. She stopped but did not turn around. "Debbie, I'm sorry," he gently said. "We need to talk. It seems that we're both running away from reality."

"Reality? I don't even know what that word means. All I know is that somewhere out there, there's a man who wants me dead. And nobody gives a damn. They all think it's a publicity stunt--even you, Dan Springer."

"Debbie--"

"Go back to your world of journalism. A world that doesn't include me!"

"Debbie, I--"

"Just go."

In spite of the fact that he was trying to be understanding, Dan felt anger nip at the edges of his nerves. If that's the way she wanted it.

He turned around and headed toward the shore, away from Debbie.

* * *

The man frantically searched for a weapon. His bare hands would not be good enough. He need something heavier. Sharper. Something that would inflict more pain.

Why had he been so stupid as not to bring anything? His eyes focused on the rocks. That's the best he could do.

For now that would be good enough.

He wondered what it would feel like to be stoned to death.

* * *

Debbie remained perfectly still, staring at Dan as he walked away from her. Then she turned to look at the stand of bushes. When she was little and living on the farm with her grandparents, and when she was lonely for Daddy, she'd walk in Grandma's garden and pretend Daddy was there with her. He'd give her advice and love her and make her feel good.

Well, maybe she could pretend again. She could pretend Dan loved her and together, hand-in-hand, they would walk through the garden, except that it wasn't a garden. But that didn't matter. It was all make believe anyway. Her entire life was enveloped in fantasy. She wasn't Debbie. She was Colette.

And everyone loved Colette.

Debbie's head hung low as she headed toward the bushes. There, seventy or eighty feet from her, her childhood garden waited.

* * *

The man felt a delightful rush of excitement. This was the moment he'd been dreaming of. For the occasion, he chose a large rock, almost four inches in diameter. He was now ready for her. His mouth watered in anticipation as he watched her heading directly toward him.

Chapter 22

Annie entered the store room where she kept her cart filled with soaps, tissues, toilet paper, pens, stationary, and various cleaning items. She reached for her purse, opened it, and retrieved Colette's picture. Softly, she began to stroke it. "You know, child," she told the picture, "even as a little girl, you always thought of me as Simple Annie. But if only you were alive now, you wouldn't call me Simple Annie any more. You'd call me Wise Annie." She put the picture back in her purse. "Yep, you'd call me Wise Annie."

Smiling, she headed for Ms. Elizabeth's office.

The receptionist, a young, slim woman, not particularly attractive, but not ugly either, smiled at Annie. "Annie," she said, "you're not thinking of cleaning up the place right now, are you?"

"Of course not. I'm here to talk to Ms. Elizabeth."

"Are you sure this is nothing your supervisor can handle?"

"No, ma'am. It must be Ms. Elizabeth."

"How about Jack Armstrong or Thomas Buller? I could page either one." She reached for the intercom button.

"No, ma'am. It must be Ms. Elizabeth."

The receptionist sighed. "I'm afraid Ms. Elizabeth is awfully busy. I don't think she'll be able to-"

"Just tell her I'm here, ma'am."

The receptionist frowned and glanced upward as though she knew it was all a waste of time. "All right," she said, "but you'll see that she won't be able to see you." She pressed the button, paging Elizabeth. "I'm sorry to disturb you, but Annie insists on seeing you. I've told her that you--"

"Send her in immediately."

The receptionist's jaw dropped an inch and Annie smiled. "You may go in," she said to Annie.

"Thank you, ma'am," Annie said as she walked toward Elizabeth's office. She opened the door without knocking.

Annie found Elizabeth sitting on the couch instead of behind her desk. She was wearing a two-piece navy-blue suit with matching high heels.

"What news do you have, Annie?"

"Not good news." Annie flopped herself down on the plush love seat opposite Elizabeth. "Now I know you wanna hear that I convinced Debbie to forget this foolishness about finding Colette's real killer. But I'm afraid she's a head-strong girl, and she's more determined than ever to try to prove that Sam Capacini didn't work alone."

Elizabeth threw her arms up in the air. "That's utter foolishness," she said. "I will not tolerate any foolishness nor allow her to taint my casino's reputation by reviving an issue that is best left alone. Anyway, what in the world ever gave her such a ridiculous idea?"

Annie shrugged. "I've tried to find out, but she's tight lipped when it comes to that. All she says is that she's gathering information."

"What kind of information?"

"I'm not quite sure either, but it has something to do with some park here in Las Vegas."

Elizabeth's eyebrows furrowed. "Which park, Annie?"

"I've forgotten which one, Ms. Elizabeth. Debbie did mention it by name, but it slipped my mind."

"I realize you're not a professional detective, Annie. But

your report is rather skimpy. What else do you have?" She glared and Annie and Annie felt herself recoil.

"That's all for now," she mumbled.

"By tomorrow, Annie, I want a complete report. I want the name of the park and what she knows about it. I also want to know what Debbie thinks she's doing and why she's doing it. Is that clear?"

"If you don't mind me saying so, that's a big order."

Elizabeth smirked. "Just see that it's done. I'll tell Jack Armstrong to help you in any way he can." Using his special phone code name, Elizabeth paged him, but CP 3A--otherwise known as Jack--didn't answer. Elizabeth tried two more times, each time with negative results. "Damn him!" she said. "What's going on?"

Annie shrugged.

"Well, I know exactly what he's up to. In the ten years Jack has been working for me, he has never once failed to answer his beeper, regardless of the time I call. This is a first, and I know exactly what he's doing." She folded her arms and angrily paced. "Let me tell you one thing: he's not going to get away with it. No one--absolutely no one--is ever going to ruin this casino."

* * *

The man hiding behind the trees smiled as he watched Debbie approach. Her head hung low, her hands were shoved deep in her pockets.

His eyes traveled down to his hands. He noticed that because he was clutching the rock so hard, his knuckles were almost white.

Now he glanced at Debbie's head. Her face. He pondered where to aim the rock. The small of her back and she might be paralyzed for life. Her face, and she'd be disfigured. Her head, and she'd slip into a coma.

He'd settle for the face. He wanted to maim her.

Hurt her.

Like she'd hurt him.

* * *

Thousands of questions reeled through Debbie's mind as she strolled through what she pretended to be her childhood garden. Her mind was so preoccupied that at first she didn't hear the faint sounds behind her.

Sounds like the crushing of leaves.

Footsteps, slowly, cautiously, following her.

Hard breathing. Like a madman's.

Debbie shook herself. She was only imagining these sounds. Still, she increased her pace.

A hoarse, harsh wind whispered her name. "Debbie."

She paused and turned, too late realizing her mistake. She saw a man, half-hidden by shadows cast by the bushes. She recognized him and opened her mouth to say something.

Then she noticed the rock.

He raised it and hurled it through the air.

She simultaneously ducked and turned, but because she tried to do two things at once, she lost her balance and fell. The rock hit her on her shoulder.

Blinding pain traveled through every nerve of her body, forcing her to her knees, then to the ground.

As she tumbled down, she screamed, "Daaaan!"

Her head hit the ground with a thud, causing blinding lights to explode in her brain.

* * *

When Dan heard his name, he immediately recognized the urgency behind the plea. *Debbie!* He felt his heart leap to his throat.

Oh, God, no! Please, no.

He broke into a run, at first moving clumsily. His mind told him that every second counted. He increased his speed and ran as if in a nightmare. He breathed hard and through his mouth.

"Debbie!" he yelled. "I'm coming. Hold on." *Please*

hold on. Don't die.

He could barely make out the shape of a man hovering over a body--Debbie's body! Fueled by sheer will, Dan's running became more energetic. His stride widened like a greyhound's. Even though his side hurt from running too fast, too long, he continued to push himself forward, praying he wasn't too late.

The man must have heard Dan coming, for he glanced in that direction, then turned to look at Debbie's limp body one last time before running away.

For a fraction of a second, Dan considered chasing the man. He felt the anger within him ready to erupt, driving him toward the stranger, wanting to hurt him, as he had hurt Debbie.

But as Dan approached Debbie's inert body, he quickly abandoned the idea. First, he must help Debbie, then worry about the stranger. As he knelt by her side, he heard a car engine start. He's getting away, Dan thought. With a quiver he could not control, he called Debbie's name.

His only answer was silence.

Exasperation racked through Dan's body. "Debbie!"

She moaned. He closed his eyes as he let out a sigh of relief. "Thank God. I thought--" He couldn't finish. "Are you all right?"

Slowly she nodded. "Dan, what--" She started to shake violently as she attempted to get up.

Dan wrapped his arms around her. "Are you sure you're okay?"

She winced in pain, but again she nodded.

Dan looked toward the direction the man had disappeared. "He's getting away," he said as he got to his feet and took off running. "I'll be back." He heard Debbie call him but he ignored her. His thoughts were only on seeking revenge.

By the time he reached the other side of the

campground, the car had already sped away. "Shit!" he said and quickly returned to Debbie's side.

He found her half-sitting, half-lying, her hands cradling her head. "Did you get a good look at him?"

She looked up at him, startled. She cleared her throat. "Well, uh, no, I don't...think so. He...it happened so fast." She looked away from Dan, toward the dirt. "No, I didn't see him."

Her answer triggered a spark of doubt in Dan's mind. "You're sure?"

She nodded, but still did not look up at him.

Chapter 23

Dan insisted on taking Debbie to the doctor in spite of her protests. The doctor checked her for dilated pupils and coordination. He didn't rule out a possible concussion so he wanted her awakened several times during the night.

As they walked out of the doctor's office, Dan said, "I'll spend the night with you," and then quickly added, "so I can wake you up." By now they had reached his car.

Debbie shook her head. It thumped painfully, but she was sure she was going to be all right. "Don't bother. I--"

"You heard what the doctor said." He closed the car door after Debbie had gotten in. Then he walked over to the driver's side and opened his door.

"I'll call Annie then," Debbie said even before Dan was all the way inside.

Dan drew back sharply, as if the words had been a physical blow. For a long time he stared at her in silence. "And if she won't do it?" he finally asked.

"She will."

"Debbie, I owe you an explanation," Dan said.

Debbie looked down and refused to answer.

"The problem is, Debbie, that I can't afford to fall in love with you."

He might as well have told her that she shouldn't breathe. The anguish she felt was like a knife stuck in her stomach, and the blade was slowly, painfully twisting. "I didn't ask you to." Debbie kept her eyes glued to the changing scenery: strip malls followed by gasoline stations, restaurants.

Dan opened his mouth to say something, but nothing came out. He closed it back again and focused his attention on the traffic around him. He tapped the steering wheel while waiting for the light to change. A few minutes later, he glanced at her and sighed. "Debbie, I have very strong feelings for you, but I'm forcing myself to ignore them."

Debbie felt as though her entire life was surrounded by glass which was slowly being shattered. No matter which way she turned, she seemed to cut herself on a sliver. "Is it because of Sexy Voice?"

The light changed and Dan drove off. "Who?"

"I called you last night and the night before and Sexy Voice answered both times."

Dan smirked and shook his head. "I'm sorry, Debbie," he said. "I was wondering if you had formed the wrong conclusion. It has taken every ounce of self-restraint I could muster not to bring it up."

"Well, is it because of her?" Debbie noticed that her voice was too high pitched.

"The first night you called, you talked to Jenny. The second time it was Wendy. As I told you, I can't afford to get emotionally involved, and I was doing a real good job at it until you showed up." Dan stopped at another red light and he kept his eyes focused on the traffic ahead of him.

Debbie noticed that sadness had engulfed Dan's face. His sparkling blue eyes lost their zest for life and his features became shrunken, momentarily making him seem much older. "Would you like to talk about it?" Debbie asked, touching his shoulder.

For a second, Dan turned to glance at Debbie, his eyes pleading for understanding. "I was married once," he said. "Her name was Linda and we had a little girl." Dan paused, waiting for a response from Debbie. None came, so he continued. "I was doing a story on the use of drugs here in Las Vegas. It was a pretty big story, and I was determined to go all the way. I could taste the fame, the glory this story would bring.

"Pete--that's my editor--he warned me. 'You're walking on thin wire,' he said, but I told him I knew what I was doing. I didn't listen to anybody. God! I didn't listen!"

Debbie, seeing that Dan was almost on the verge of tears, patted his shoulder. "Dan, you don't have to do this."

"Yes, I do, Debbie." He stopped and waited for some jaywalking gamblers to cross the street. They carried their buckets filled with coins. "I want to share this with you." He sighed and continued, "Finally the big day came. The first article in the series came out. I rushed home to show it to Linda..."

* * *

Dan was surprised to find the front door opened. Ever since the baby's birth, Linda had been extra careful to bolt the door after Dan left. But not today.

"Linda!" Dan said, not expecting an answer. He assumed she had taken the baby and had gone next door.

As soon as he shut the door behind him, a feeling of foreboding gnawed at his insides. "Linda?" he said again, but this time more carefully as though afraid of the answer.

As soon as he stepped away from the entry hall and into the living room, his mind froze with a sudden jolt of fear. The couch had been overturned. Books and magazines were strewn across the floor creating a chaotic mess. A lamp had been thrown clear across the room, and its scattered remains bore evidence of a violent struggle.

For minutes he stared at the living room, unable to wrench his eyes from each abhorring detail. Involuntarily, a short moan, like that made by a man who had suddenly lost all his wind, escaped from his throat.

Innumerable thoughts roared at him as his eyes focused

on the small red stains around the room. *Blood! My God! That's blood!* Suddenly the blood stains screamed at him. "Linda!" he shouted as he dashed upstairs. He bounded two, three steps at a time.

But even before he reached the top, he saw his wife's body sprawled on the floor halfway between their bedroom and the hallway. She had obviously been dragging herself down the hall toward Diana's room. But now she lay still--very still-- her face buried in the carpet.

Dan took a short step forward while his mind ordered him to run toward her. Yet, he wanted to remain glued to the floor. He didn't want to know, didn't want to touch her.

Run! She may be alive. She has to be alive.

Without realizing he had moved, Dan found himself kneeling next to his wife's body. "Linda," he whispered as he rolled her over. He gasped as he stared in horror at Linda's blood-smeared face.

But in spite of the blood he could see her eyelids flicker. *She's alive! SHE'S ALIVE! I must get help.* He started to set her down but her lips formed the word "No."

"You're going to be all right," Dan found himself saying this, wanting with all his heart to believe it. "I'm going to call emergency."

"No--no time." It seemed like hours passed before she was able to form the next word, "Diana?"

"She's okay. She's in her room. She's safe." *Diana! Where was she? How was she?*

Linda's eyes formed a smile. "I...love you." She closed her eyes.

"I . . . love . . . you too." He kissed her forehead, her cheek, her lips. He held her tightly and rocked her. "I will always love you. Always . . . always." The lump in his throat grew to the size of a lemon.

He gently set her back down, and his thoughts turned to Diana--*Diana!* He ran to the baby's room, tears fogging his vision. He pushed the door open. The room was neat--and empty. Dan stood in the doorway, thinking...thinking.

The sudden ringing of the phone sent a shock wave through his body. Maybe he should just let it ring. But it could be...them. His feet scraped the carpet as he dragged himself to the den. With robot-type movements he reached for the receiver. "Yes?"

"We have Diana."

"You son-of-a-bitch! If you so much as touch one hair--"

"If you want her back, listen." The voice was raspy, obviously disguised.

Dan felt all energy drain from him. "I'm listening." He recognized the defeat in his voice.

"Kill the series or we'll kill her."

"How do I know you really have her? Or if she's alive?"

"You don't, but do you want to take that chance?" The phone went dead, but not before he heard a baby's cry in the background.

* * *

"And your daughter?" Debbie asked. They had reached the casino's parking lot, but they remained in the car, the windows rolled down as it was hot.

"I've never found her." Dan's voice sounded hollow.

"That's why you stare at all the little girls," Debbie said.

"I do?" Dan nodded. "I guess I do. It hurts so much not knowing if she's alive or abused or loved." He hung his head and his lips trembled. "She would be six now." He shook his head. "Six years. Every year that passes--every second--it makes it that much harder to find her."

"Don't you have a lot of friends in the police department? Can't they help?"

"Every policeman in Las Vegas carries an age-progression picture of Diana. They questioned and detained men whom we know had information on my daughter's whereabouts. The police threatened them with real and fake charges. Nothing worked. In the end, they all had to be released."

"Does that mean the police have given up finding Diana?"

"I guess if it was up to them, they would have. But I can't blame them. Every lead we've had has been a dead-end, but I won't let them file this away. I check with them every week. I don't know if it does any good, but at least I know that it's keeping the case right on the very top of their files."

"Is there anything I can do?"

"I wish there was. Right now my best bets are my informers. I got them strung out all over the state and some in other strategic places."

"Any luck with them?"

Dan smirked. "I found and re-united two girls with their families. The parents cried and thanked me, and do you know what was going through my mind both times?"

"What?"

"Why them? Why not me? As they were thanking me and hugging me, I was hating them." His eyes watered and he wiped away the tears with angry movements.

Debbie reached out for him. "No, Debbie," he said. "I don't deserve happiness, and I'll only bring you misery. Now you know why I won't let myself love you. Everyone I touch, I hurt."

"Dan, that's--"

"Sh." He reached for the door. "Let's call Annie."

Chapter 24

"Wanna talk about it, child?" Annie asked. They were sitting in Debbie's suite. Annie had brought out a pitcher of freshly made juice and poured Debbie a large glass.

"Aren't you going to have any?" Debbie asked. "There's plenty for both of us."

"I never touch that stuff. It's nasty," Annie said as she handed Debbie her glass.

Smiling, Debbie took a large gulp and looked up at Annie.

"You have problems opening up to people, huh, child?"

Debbie nodded.

"Don't fret. You don't have to tell me anything you don't want."

"It isn't that," Debbie said.

"Then what, child?"

Debbie stared at her juice and drank over half-a-glass.

Annie reached out and squeezed her hand. "While you're figuring out if you want to tell me or not, can I tell you something that is bothering me?"

"Of course."

"First, let me tell you that I have no idea why this bothers me. Maybe it's because I have been working here for so long. I feel it's my casino too. You know what I mean?"

Debbie nodded.

"Now you swear you're not going to tell? I could get into plenty of trouble for this."

Annie had piqued Debbie's curiosity. "What is it, Annie?"

Annie glanced all around her as though the room was filled with listening people. She leaned toward Debbie and whispered, "You heard that Ms. Elizabeth found her sister."

Debbie nodded. "Dan told me when he was here interviewing Ms. Elizabeth."

"During that interview, did he find out that she's not her sister?" Annie reached over and refilled Debbie's glass.

"What do you mean, Annie?"

"Simply that I've known this woman since we were babies and there's no way she's Ms. Elizabeth's long lost sister."

"My God, Annie, why would Ms. Elizabeth do something like that?"

"I'm not sure. But I bet you it's got something to do with what she told Colette once."

"Which was?"

Annie shrugged. "Colette never told me. All I know is that after Colette and Ms. Elizabeth talked, Colette was very upset for a long time."

Debbie leaned back on the couch. Suddenly she was starting to feel very sleepy. "Do you have the slightest idea what they talked about?"

"Colette made some references to Ms. Elizabeth's sister, but back then I had no idea what she was talking about." Annie refilled Debbie's juice glass. "Now, I know you work closely with Dan. You can tell him. He can help you sort this out, and maybe you can get to the bottom."

"Do you really think..." She yawned. God, she felt so sleepy. "...Ms. Elizabeth's sister has something to do with me?"

"It had something to do with Colette, and somehow

you're connected with Colette."

"But how?"

Annie shrugged. "I'm not sure. There's much I don't know."

Debbie leaned back on the couch and rested her head against its back. "It started with a phone call," she began and continued on until she got to the part about her experience at the lake.

"At first I thought I had just imagined the noise." Debbie reached for her juice and drained its contents. "But as I walked a couple of feet more, I could tell that someone was out there. I was going to run--I really was. I was going to run away from him." Debbie felt as though her stomach had turned, and she knew any minute now she would cry. "Then I did something stupid, Annie."

Annie reached out and held Debbie's hands. "Sh, child. It's over now." She refilled Debbie's glass.

"I wish..." A tremor shook her body. "I wish it was. But it's just a beginning." Her lower lip trembled, and she breathed through her mouth. "I turned to look at him. Oh, God, I wish I hadn't done that. I saw him, Annie. I saw him!"

"Who, Debbie? Who was it?"

"I don't know."

Annie's eyebrows knit slightly in puzzlement. "What do you mean: you don't know?"

"When I saw him, I recognized him. I know I did! But afterward--after Dan was with me--I couldn't remember." Debbie felt her mouth dry. She reached for her juice and played with the rim of the glass. "It's like waking up from a dream. You can remember what happened just as soon as you wake up, but a second later..." Debbie snapped her fingers. "...it's all gone."

Annie shook her head. "You gotta remember. It's important, child. Now think!"

"I've tried, but I can't." Debbie felt so sleepy that she

had trouble getting the words out. "I want very much to remember..."

"Do you?"

"Of course, but no matter how much I try, it's as if it never really happened." Debbie felt her head drop. She immediately jerked it back up again, forcing her eyes to open wide. "I'm so sleepy." She fought to stay awake.

"Debbie, listen to me!" Annie grabbed Debbie by the shoulder and shook her. "If you want me to help ya, I need to know. Who was it you saw?"

"Tomorrow," Debbie whispered, "after I've had a chance to think some more." Even to her own ears, her words sounded slurred.

"Was it Jack Armstrong?"

Debbie stared at Annie, her mind unable to comprehend

Annie grabbed Debbie's arms and shook her. "Tell me, child. It's very important. I have to know. Was it Jack Armstrong?"

"I'm so...sleepy," Debbie said. She folded her arm on the couch's side, then rested her head on top of her arm. Her eyes closed even as she lowered her head.

Chapter 25

The vaguely familiar noise reached Debbie as though it were coming from a different dimension. She tried to ignore it, but to her dismay, the noise persisted. She focused her attention on it. It was...it was...the ringing of a phone.

Debbie's eyes snapped opened. For a second, she felt disoriented, groggy. Where was she? Debbie looked around. She was in her room, safe in bed. Just a few minutes ago she had been talking to Annie. How-when-had she gone to bed? Debbie blinked several times trying to focus her vision, trying to clear her head.

Coming more to her senses, Debbie realized that the phone was still ringing. She reached for it. "Hello?"

"Debbie."

Debbie held her breath in anticipation. She had thought she and Dan were through after last night. "Hi, Dan."

"I've been worried sick about you," he said.

"Worried? Why?"

"I've been calling since early this morning, and there was no answer. You missed your aerobics class, your breakfast publicity and rehearsal."

Debbie's head swivelled toward the alarm clock. It was twelve-thirty-one. Was it really possible? Had she actually slept the morning away? "I don't have rehearsal today or tomorrow. Bill wants to work with the current show--some kind of a problem he wants to correct."

"Good, in that case why don't you join me for lunch? I've got some news for you."

Debbie looked down and noticed that she was still dressed in yesterday's clothes. "Yeah, sure," she said. "I'm already dressed."

"Great!" Dan said. "I'm down here in the casino. I'll be up in less than five minutes."

Debbie bolted out of bed and began to change.

* * *

When Debbie went to answer the door, she noticed a piece of paper laying close to the front door. She bent down and picked it up. It was a blank, sealed envelope. She clutched it as she swung the door open.

A frown replaced Dan's smile. "What's wrong?" He stepped inside.

She handed him the envelope.

"Where did you get that?"

"I just found it," she said. "Right now. It was right there." She pointed to the floor.

"Do you want me to read it?"

Debbie nodded, and she placed her opened hands on her chest, like a heroine of the silent movies.

Dan ripped the corner of the envelope and moved closer so Debbie could also see. He flashed her a reassuring smile and took out the sheet of paper. He unfolded it and read it aloud:

The missing piece to Colette's death puzzle lies in Waltman Park. Go there for the answer.

The unsigned note had been typed on a plain piece of white bond paper.

"What is this about?" Dan asked.

"You know as much about it as I do," Debbie answered. "But I'll tell you one thing: there's no doubt in my mind that someone definitely wants me to find Colette's murderer."

"I agree. I just wish I knew who it was."

"You find that answer, and you find the person who wants me dead."

"Not necessarily." Dan sat down on the recliner facing the couch. "We could be looking at two different persons: the one who wants you to find the murderer, and the one who doesn't."

"Dan, I know you came here so we could have lunch, but I'd really rather go to the park." Debbie sat down on the couch and wished Dan had chosen to sit by her.

"That's not a good idea. It could be a trap. You're not going to the park."

"But, Dan--"

Dan raised his hand, signifying the end of the conversation. "Don't worry. I'll go, and if I find anything there, I'll let you know."

"Dan, you're welcome to come with me if you want, but I'm going."

Dan frowned. "What about having some lunch first?"

"I'm not really hungry. In fact, my stomach is kind of upset. Why don't I just make a sandwich in here?"

Dan nodded and followed Debbie toward the kitchen. As they walked past the dining room Debbie noticed that the pitcher of juice and the half-empty glass she had used last night had not been put away. She shrugged and made a mental note to ask Annie why she hadn't put them up.

"What kind of sandwich would you like?" Debbie asked sticking her head in the refrigerator.

"Do you have ham and cheese?"

"Yep."

"That's my favorite."

"And to drink?"

"Coke is fine."

Debbie gathered all of the items and set them on top of the counter.

"What are you having?"

"I think I'll just drink some juice."

Dan smiled. "You really are hooked on that stuff."

"Orange juice? Yeah, I love it," Debbie said as she popped two slices of bread into the toaster. "You should have seen me last night. I must have drunk five or six glasses--big ones too. Annie and I were talking and she just kept on pouring and pouring."

"And?"

"And nothing. I just drank it. That's all." She stopped slicing the tomato and stared at Dan. "It was the strangest thing. I remember sitting there talking to Annie, drinking that juice. The next thing I remember is waking up when you called."

"Didn't Annie stay with you?"

Debbie shrugged. "I suppose she did. I don't know."

"Didn't she wake you up like she was supposed to?"

"I don't think so. If she did, I don't remember." She picked up the tomato and resumed slicing it. "And that's very unusual."

"How's that?"

"I have always been a very light sleeper, and I have never slept late."

"Except for this morning. I must have called at least four, five times before you answered."

"Maybe yesterday I did get a concussion, huh?"

"The doctor didn't seem to think so." Dan glanced at the pitcher of orange juice. "Tell me, did Annie drink any of that juice?"

"No, she told me that she hates orange juice. Why?"

He picked up the pitcher and smelled it. He poured himself a small glass and took a tiny sip.

"What are you doing?" Debbie asked. She momentarily stopped preparing the sandwich and stared at Dan.

"Is this last night's juice?"

"I guess so."

"You're very sure?"

"No, I'm not sure at all, but why would Annie dump perfectly good...juice?" She paused, startled. "You don't think Annie put anything in there, do you?"

"She might have."

"But why?"

"I don't know. But until we solve this, everyone is a suspect."

"Can't you take some juice and go get it tested for drugs?"

"I can and I will. But I'm willing to bet that if Annie did drug you, she dumped out the left-over juice, washed everything, and made out a new batch. I just wish I could find out if she did."

"You might be able to."

"Oh?"

"I had two cans of frozen orange juice left. I know because I wanted to tell Annie I was running low. If there are still two cans there, then there's a chance that we're just being paranoid."

Debbie headed toward the refrigerator and Dan followed her. Without hesitating, she opened the door.

There was only one can of orange juice left.

Chapter 26

"I still can't believe that Annie would drug me." Debbie was applying her Colette make-up.

Dan had taken his sandwich and Coke into Debbie's bedroom and sat on the bed, eating and watching Debbie. He seemed relaxed, but Debbie felt her nerves tingle. She still remembered last night.

"She might not have," Dan answered. "You did get a nasty bump on your head yesterday."

"Yeah, let's hope that's all it was." She reached for her eye shadow. "You said you had something to tell me."

"I dropped by Richard Steven's office." Dan took a large bite of his sandwich.

"Who?"

"Richard Steven. He's a real estate agent who specializes in handwriting analysis. When he isn't busy selling real estate, he's at the police department analyzing handwriting for them, either professionally or for fun."

"What did he have to say?" Debbie blotted the excess lipstick with a Kleenex.

"Unfortunately, nothing," Dan wiped his mouth and

gulped down some Coke. "He wasn't there, but I did leave the two envelopes and letters you gave me and put them inside his top drawer. I should be hearing from him sometime this afternoon. Then we'll know whether or not it was your director who sent you both of the letters."

Debbie closed her eyes, attempting to shut the world off. So much was happening. She wondered if she'd be able to sort it all out. "I also have some news for you," she said, "which may mean something or nothing at all."

"Oh? What's that?" Dan set the empty plate on top of Debbie's dresser, then drank the last of his Coke.

"Annie told me that the woman Ms. Elizabeth claims is her long-lost sister isn't really her sister at all."

Dan let some air out through his mouth. "I kinda had a hunch about the same thing. As a reporter, I would be most interested in finding out what she's up to."

"Ms. Elizabeth needed to produce a sister in order to meet the qualifications under her father's new will. What we need to do is find out who the real sister is. Too bad Mr. Lovingsworth died. He'd be the one to talk to."

"We could go for second best."

"Ms. Elizabeth, you mean?"

"I don't think Ms. Elizabeth would be very cooperative, do you?"

"No, I guess not. But who then?"

"Mr. Lovingsworth's personal maid. Not the one he just had, but the one he had while Ms. Elizabeth was growing up."

"It sounds good to me, but how do we know who that was?"

"You're going to the Personnel Department."

Debbie frowned. "I thought I was going to the park."

"You will, but if it's a trap, you'll fall right into it by going now. If you make them wait, they'll get nervous and hopefully, sloppy."

Debbie considered this for a moment. "All right. I'll go

to the Personnel Office first. What am I suppose to do there?"

"There's a red-headed woman who'll be looking for you. Her name is Paula Wiant. She'll take you to the proper file cabinet so you can go through it."

"Why can't she do it herself?"

"Because she's afraid she'll get caught. She says her job is very important to her. In fact, she made me promise that if you get caught, you'll keep her name out of it."

"I can do that, but if that happens, what should I do?"

"Tell them you were looking for your file. You were curious as to what was in it. I know that's weak, but at least it's an excuse." He reached across the table and held Debbie's hand. "I don't like the idea of you going, but I can't do it. Everyone in there knows I'm a reporter. There's no way I could get near the files. Will you do it?"

Debbie looked up at Dan and their eyes locked. She nodded.

* * *

Debbie found the Personnel Office housed on the seventh floor of the Crystal Palace Casino. Double-doors led to a small waiting room. A long counter separated it from the rest of the office area. Behind the counter, the place buzzed with ringing phones. Several women pounded information into the computer keyboard.

As soon as Debbie stepped in, a red-headed woman with a round face came running up to her. "Excuse me, aren't you Debbie Gunther?"

Debbie nodded.

"Hi! My name is Paula Wiant. I just love to watch you perform. You're so good."

"Thank you very much, Paula. I appreciate that." She looked around the office and whispered, "Are you--"

"Yes, I am, Dan told me you'd be coming." She started walking toward the back of the room. Debbie followed her. "Did Dan tell you I don't want anything to do with this?"

"Don't worry. We'll keep you out of it if I get caught, but I won't."

Paula paused and her tongue flickered nervously over her lips. "What exactly is it you want?"

"I'm looking for--"

Paula waved her hand in the air. "Don't be too specific. I don't want to know. The less I know the better."

Wonderful. Paula was going to be a lot of help. If Debbie had a gun she'd go shoot Dan right now. She wasn't cut out for this cloak and dagger stuff. "I need to see who was working here say about thirty years ago."

Paula's eyes narrowed. She pointed with her head toward a closed door to her right. "The files are kept in there, in the restricted area. Only Ms. Elizabeth and Personnel Managers are allowed in there."

"Aren't you a manager?"

"Of course I am."

"Well, then?"

"You're not..." Paula stopped. "Oh, what the hell. It isn't like there's any big secrets in there. Just a bunch of job applications. Besides, I did promise Dan I'd help you." She looked around at her co-workers. They were all engrossed in their own work. "Come on," she said.

Once inside the file room, Debbie took a quick glance around the room. It contained at least forty-to-fifty four-drawer file cabinets.

"That's a lot of files," Debbie said. "How could you ever find anything?"

"It's very simple. It's filed by year as well as by occupation. If you know what you're looking for, you can pinpoint it in a matter of seconds. It's just a simple case of knowing which file cabinet is which, and luckily for you, each file cabinet is labeled."

Debbie began to walk down the rows of cabinets. She noticed that the most recent years were toward the front.

"I'm going to leave you now," Paula said. "Remember--"

Debbie put her extended index finger on top of her lips. "I know. Not a word."

Paula flashed a weak smile then turned to leave. And just as she did, the door opened and Elizabeth stepped in.

Chapter 27

The look of panic in Paula's face registered in Debbie's mind. She knew that Paula's job was on the line, and it was up to her to save her.

Luckily, Elizabeth had not yet noticed them. Debbie quickly hid between two cabinets and gently pushed Paula toward Ms. Elizabeth. She told her with her eyes to get rid of Ms. Elizabeth.

Paula picked up on the hint. She headed directly toward her. "Ms. Elizabeth, is there a file I can get for you?"

Elizabeth paused for a second, obviously startled. "Paula, what are you doing here?"

"I came over here to pick up some more files to enter in the computer."

"I thought Cheryl and Pat were doing that."

"They are. But I'm pretty much caught up with my work so I figured I could enter a couple of files."

Elizabeth nodded and continued to head toward the general area where Debbie was crouched between the cabinets. "So where's your files?"

"I haven't gotten them yet. I was going to do that, but then I heard the door open. Since I'm getting mine, is there a file I can get for you?"

Elizabeth stopped. "Yes, as a matter of fact, there is."

"Why don't we go to my office and you can fill me in?" Paula began to lead Elizabeth out.

Debbie waited several seconds after they left before she came out of her hiding place. Not wanting to lose any more time, she scurried past the rows of file cabinets, her eyes searching for what she hoped was the correct year.

When she found it, she quickly tried to open it. It was locked. She tried the other three doors. They were also locked. "Damn!" she said.

She opened her purse and retrieved the small file Dan had given her. He had spent over an hour teaching her how to pick a lock. He had made her practice several times until she could open the cabinets within seconds.

Now, here she was facing her real challenge, not knowing if she could pull it through. She inserted the file, turned it, and tried the drawer. It was still locked.

"Concentrate!" she told herself. She pretended she was back in Dan's office and he was standing next to her, giving her instructions. She tried it once again. This time she was successful.

The first drawer contained V.I.P. personnel records such as managers, supervisors. The second drawer housed less important positions: casino runners, waiters, card dealers. The third drawer was the janitorial drawer. Debbie quickly scanned through the files. No one had been hired that year to be Mr. Lovingsworth's personal maid.

She closed the drawers and moved on down to the next file cabinet. Again, she was unsuccessful. She wasn't any luckier with the next two file cabinets.

She moved down to the next one. Half-way through the file, she came across the right information. One of the employees who had been with the casino for the past five years had been promoted. She was to become Mr. Lovingsworth's personal maid.

Debbie quickly took out her note pad and copied down

the name: Marianne Anderson. Beside it, she wrote down the address and phone number.

She put the file back, then decided she'd better look over one more time just in case she had missed something important. Noticing nothing out of the ordinary, she put the file back.

Behind her, she heard a harsh voice call her name.

Startled, Debbie looked up.

Chapter 28

"Paula!" Debbie said. "You scared me." She slammed the drawer shut and stood up. "Is it safe to go out?"

Paula nodded. "Are you finished?"

"Yes, thank you very much."

"I wish I could say it was no problem, but the truth is I'm scared shitless. Let's get you out of here before somebody else comes in."

* * *

Mrs. Anderson turned out to be a seventy-six year-old widow who in spite of her years seemed very alert. She offered Dan and Debbie some coffee and the three of them sat down in her cramped living room, which consisted of one worn-out sofa and a wide screen television set.

After sipping her coffee, Mrs. Anderson said, "I'm so glad you came, Mr....uh..."

"Springer. Dan Springer. And this is my associate, Debbie Gunther."

"Debbie Gunther, eh?" Mrs. Anderson scratched her chin. "You look mighty familiar."

"A lot of people say I look like Colette," Debbie said.

"Who?"

"Colette, the movie star."

"Oh, yes, I remember her. Got killed, didn't she?"

"Yes," Debbie said.

"Nope," Mrs. Anderson shook her head.

"I beg your pardon," Debbie said.

"That's not who I was thinkin' you remind me of." She leaned back, even though it took up more space in the already crowded couch. "But it'll come to me." She smacked her lips. "It'll come." Then, as though pulling herself away from the deep thoughts she had, she said, "I'm glad you all came. I don't have any more friends at the casino. I understand they have a whole new crew now. I never talk to them. I miss the ol' crowd. Our little pleasures came from getting together and gossipin'. You learn a lot about the casino that way, you know. The stars--the famous people--those were our favorite subjects."

"What about Mr. Lovingsworth?"

"What about him?"

"Did you ever hear any gossip about him?"

Marianne covered her mouth with both hands. "Oh, goodness, no! That was strictly forbidden. He was my employer, you know. I was his personal maid. To keep a job like that you must keep your eyes and ears--and especially your mouth--shut. Oh, no, goodness, no. No gossip there. Never!"

Dan leaned forward. "But still you must have known some of the gossip."

Marianne eyed him suspiciously. "What is it that you want, Mr. Dan Springer?"

"I need your help in locating Ms. Elizabeth's sister."

Marianne's forehead wrinkled. "I saw it on the teevee where she had already found her sister."

"We have reason to believe that she is not really Ms. Elizabeth's sister."

Marianne rubbed her hands together. "Oh, this is good. Real good. Tell me about it. But no, wait. I made a delicious carrot cake, and I hardly ever get a chance to share my cooking talents with others."

With an agility which surprised both Dan and Debbie, she was gone. She returned with three huge slices and coffee for the three of them. "Now tell me why this lady is not really Ms. Elizabeth's sister."

"We're not sure if she is or isn't," Dan said as he stirred his coffee. "We're just checking, so please keep this visit confidential."

"I will," Marianne said, "and more out of necessity rather than by choice. You're the first company I've had in months." She took a big bite out of her cake. "So tell me, what can I do for you?"

"We were wondering if you by any chance remember a certain lady Mr. Lovingsworth was always with?"

"Someone other than his wife, you mean." She smiled.

Dan nodded. "Was there someone like that?"

"Oh, yes, there most certainly was. But I'm afraid she's not the one you're looking for."

"Oh?'

"The person I'm referring to is Ms. Elizabeth herself. She was little kid back them. Eight, maybe nine, and her father had already started her education, as he put it. That's all he ever talked to her about as though that's the only thing in life that mattered." Marianne paused and looked at the ceiling as though remembering. "It doesn't surprise me that Ms. Elizabeth never got married, the way her father drilled her over and over. Business, always business." She frowned. "I think, Mr. Dan Springer, that's a real shame, don't you?"

Dan nodded and made a face at Debbie, as though telling her that information seldom came easily. "Are you sure there was no one else besides Ms. Elizabeth?"

"Very sure. Mr. Lovingsworth never mixed business with pleasure. In fact, I don't even remember seeing much of Mrs. Lovingsworth."

"In all those years you worked for him you never saw

him with another woman?"

"Oh, I didn't say that, Mr. Dan Springer. He was always with a beautiful woman--but not a woman, but women. It was part of the business, you know. I couldn't begin to tell you if one of those is the one you want." She sighed, folded her hands and placed them on her lap. "Not much help, was I?"

Dan smiled. "If you happen to remember anything, I'd appreciate it if you call me." He took out his business card and handed it to her.

"I most surely will." She briefly glanced at the card then back up at Dan. "I have a whole bunch of pictures both of you may be interested in looking at. They're of the famous people who came to the casino. I wasn't supposed to take those pictures, you know. I could have gotten into a lot of trouble if they ever found out. That was a strict casino rule: 'No photographs.' But I took 'em anyway. Snapped more than my share. I got lots of famous people--all the ones who played at the casino while I was there." She stood up and with the vigor of a child, she treaded over to the front closet. "I got a box full over here. Let me show them to you."

Dan pushed his empty plate away, wiped his mouth, and stood up. "That's very sweet, Mrs. Anderson, but I'm afraid we can't. We still have another person to see." Dan helped Debbie up.

"Oh, nonsense, Mr. Dan Springer. Indulge me and make an old lady happy." She turned to Debbie. "You, Ms. Debbie Gunther, make him listen to me."

Feeling trapped and not wanting to be rude, Debbie smiled and sat down again. "We can't stay long," she said.

Dan also sat down. "All right, just a few pictures. Then we'll have to leave before we're late for our next appointment."

Dan and Debbie looked at picture after picture. The ones of Elizabeth as a little girl held some interest, but overall, Mrs. Anderson's valued memories were of no importance to Debbie, and, judging by Dan's expression, they weren't important to him either. Debbie recognized several movie stars, and she grinned at the knowledge of how these stars would be upset if they could see these unflattering pictures.

"Here's one," Marianne said as she picked still another picture. "It's Ms. Elizabeth and her father. She was ten years old and looks upset because--" Suddenly her face brightened as she snapped her fingers. "I think I got something for you. I just remembered. This picture-" She waved it in the air. "-made me remember."

Dan stared at the picture, then handed it to Debbie. The father was bending down, whispering something in Elizabeth's ear. Elizabeth was pouting, her eyes shone with anger.

"If gossip has it right, it seems that Ms. Elizabeth showed up at the casino unexpectedly. She walked right into her father's office without knocking. She caught him kissin' a lady who was not her mother. She took off runnin' and Mr. Lovingsworth went after her. I never did find out what he told her. I always wish I had. I asked everybody I knew, but if they knew, they were pretty tight lipped. Do you know what I mean?"

Dan nodded and asked, "Do you remember who this lady was?"

"Nope, I only saw her once or twice at the very most. Like I said, Mr. Lovingsworth did not like to combine business and pleasure."

"Do you remember her name?" Dan leaned forward, listening intently.

She shook her head. "Never knew it."

Dan frowned. "Do you remember anything that could help us? For example, what she looked like?"

"I can do better." She searched through the picture box. "I took her picture. I figured it might be valuable one day. Maybe that day is finally here. Don't you think so, Mr. Dan Springer?" Her forehead furrowed as she continued to search.

After a few minutes, she pulled one out, "Ah, here it is!" She handed it to Dan.

Dan's mouth dropped open as he stared at the picture. His reaction aroused Debbie's curiosity. She wanted to grab the picture away from him. Common sense told her not to look. Cautiously she asked, "Do you know her?"

"Maybe," Dan said slowly, and handed the picture to Debbie.

Debbie stared at the woman with a familiar face--a woman who, with a different hairdo and modern clothes, could easily pass as Debbie Gunther herself. "Who is she?" Debbie asked.

"She looks awfully familiar," Dan said. He looked at Marianne. "Do you, by any chance, know her name or know of somebody who would know her name?"

Marianne wrinkled her face, making her look like a prune. "No, sorry."

"Mind if I keep the picture?" When Marianne didn't answer, Dan quickly added, "I'll take very good care of it and I promise that I'll return it as soon as possible."

Marianne nodded.

Chapter 29

It was a few minutes past four o'clock when Debbie and Dan returned to Debbie's suite. Immediately, Debbie headed for the phone. "Excuse me for a second, Dan. I need to call Jack Armstrong. I should have done it a long time ago."

When the receiver was picked up, she identified herself and asked to speak to Jack. "I don't know what to tell him." Debbie looked up at Dan as she waited for Jack to be paged.

"Tell him the truth. Tell him you overslept."

"He'll never accept that as an excuse. I'll just tell him that something really important came up." She heard the phone being picked up. "Jack, I--"

"I don't want to hear it. But I do want you to know that, like a fool, I covered for you." Jack Armstrong's voice came harshly over the phone. "I told the reporters that my secretary made a mistake and she set up the publicity meal for seven in the evening, instead of seven in the morning. I apologized profusely and told them you would be there tonight. And you *will* be there."

"Yes, of course, I will be there."

"I'm very glad to hear that, because if you are even one second late, you can find a new job. Tonight, I expect a perfect Colette." He slammed the phone down.

Still holding the receiver, Debbie turned to Dan. "I think he was upset."

Dan shrugged. "That happens sometimes." He looked at his wrist watch. "I need to get going. I want to stop by Richard's and see if he's had a chance to analyze that handwriting. I also want to stop by the police and talk to their artist."

"Why?"

"I'm going to give him that picture Marianne let us borrow. I'll ask him to age it."

Debbie wrinkled her forehead in a puzzled expression.

"You know, project what the lady in the picture would look like now. If we're lucky, we'll recognize her."

"I hope so," Debbie said, nodding.

"Also, since you'll be tied up with Jack, I'll try to drop by the park. If I find anything, I'll call you. Otherwise, why don't we meet for breakfast tomorrow at eight-thirty--that is provided that you don't oversleep."

Debbie stuck her tongue out at him. "Smart ass," she said.

* * *

As soon as Debbie entered the elegant Crystal Dining Room, she spotted Jack Armstrong, but she didn't head directly toward him. Instead she stood in the entry doorway a little longer than necessary, flashed a giant smile, waved at Jack, and slowly began heading his way. Debbie knew that would have been the way Colette entered a room, and Jack had specifically asked Debbie to impersonate Colette to the smallest of details.

Jack stood up and greeted her, gently kissing her cheek. As he helped her with her chair he whispered in her ear between clenched teeth, "I know you went on a picnic yesterday and again you wore jeans. Colette would have never lowered herself that way."

Anger invaded Debbie's mind. "I have a perfect right--"

"Smile." Jack flashed a smile. "Everybody in here is watching you. You're the star. You blow it now, baby, and you're through.   Not just here, but in Hollywood and New York."   Still smiling, he raised his champagne glass as in a toast.

Debbie wrinkled her nose and slightly threw her head back, just as Colette would have done.   Now-and-then a camera flashed, and Debbie posed and smiled.

When the waiter came, Debbie ordered an assortment of fresh fruits.

"I like that," Jack said.   "You ordered exactly what Colette would have ordered. You've done your homework. I am impressed."

"Thank you. I do believe in being thorough."

A waiter, carrying a pot filled with hot, freshly brewed coffee, approached their table.   Jack waited until he had refilled his cup before he began to speak. "The man sitting at the table next to us is Harry Watkins. He's a multi-billionaire with a lot of influences. He's my special guest. In a few minutes, I want you to glance his way, hold his eye for a minute then give him one of your extra-sexy smiles. Then ignore him for the rest of the meal."

A platter filled with various types of fruits arrived. Debbie helped herself to some, signed some autographs, then glanced toward Harry Watkins. She immediately recognized him "Jack, I know that man."

Jack stiffened. "What do you mean?"

"He's been following me and watching me. It just seems that every place I go, he's there--and sometimes he's there ahead of me, as if he knows my schedule." She felt her flesh tingle.

"Well, I wouldn't worry about it. He's a very rich man, so naturally he will show up at the same places you would. What I want you to do now is stop looking his way so much," Jack said. "But the next time you do, wink."

Debbie's eyes drifted from Jack to the stranger. For a second their eyes met, and she gave him a coquettish wink and looked away. Through the remainder of the meal, Debbie ignored him, but still she could feel his eyes analyzing her. By the time Jack and Debbie finished their leisurely supper, Harry had already left.

"What now?" Debbie asked, as she very carefully dabbed at the corner of her mouth with her lace-rimmed napkin.

"Now there's a reception for V.I.P.'s only. Then you're to make yourself very visible downstairs for at least an hour."

* * *

While Debbie was thus occupied, a man let himself into Debbie's suite. He walked around her living room, dragging his hand on top of the soft couch. He stared at the chandelier, the expensive knick knacks. "Nice," he said. "That bitch doesn't deserve this!"

He walked around the kitchen, the dining room, mentally noticing all of the extras this suite contained. Then he went into her bedroom, opened the closet, and examined her clothes. He opened up the drawers and stared at her sexy underwear. "Bitch! Bitch! Bitch!" he yelled. He returned to her closet and pulled down the box Debbie had on the top shelf. He opened it and smiled when he saw Poo Bear. He took the stuffed animal out and banged it against the dresser. He pulled its arms and legs and ripped its clothes. Feeling exhausted, he wandered aimlessly around the living room. He paused when he heard Debbie out in the hallway.

* * *

Debbie stood outside of her suite, fishing for her keys from the bottom of her purse, when she heard someone call her. She turned and saw Jack approaching.

"Debbie, I just came to tell you that you were wonderful tonight. You generated a lot of interest." He extended out his hand and Debbie shook it. "Congratulations on a job well done."

"Thanks, Jack." She waited to see if he had anything

else to say.

Picking up the hint, Jack said, "That's all I wanted to say. A couple of high rollers are hitting the tables tonight. I need to go make unscheduled rounds." He started to turn, but at the last minute stopped. "Just remember, now more than ever, Colette all the way." He put his thumb up.

Debbie watched him turn the corner, shrugged, and continued to search for her keys. That's when she noticed that her door was unlocked. She turned to call for Jack, but he was gone.

Without stepping in she pushed the door open and peeked inside. "Annie?" She stepped inside. Everything seemed normal. Nothing unusual. She had probably opened the door herself while she was talking to Jack, and she hadn't even noticed it.

With deliberate slowness, Debbie walked to the phone and picked it up. She dialed Dan's home phone.

The phone rang once.

Please answer!

Twice.

Debbie's eyes scanned her living room.

The phone continued to ring and on about the seventh ring while Debbie's eyes still darted from object to object, she noticed something unusual: the door to her bedroom was open a third of the way. She always closed it. *Annie. Annie must have been here to clean the suite. She must have left it open.*

Debbie slammed the phone down, her eyes still glued to her bedroom door. For a few seconds her hand lingered a bit on the receiver, but her eyes refused to move away from the door. It were as if any minute now Debbie was expecting the door to grow fangs. Slowly she walked toward it. She could feel the perspiration beads form on the top of her lip.

As she inched her way around the couch, heading toward the door, a small bundle scattered on the floor caught her attention. At first it looked like nothing more than a pile of cleaning rags, but as she carefully approached it, it began to take a definite shape. She saw an eye, a nose, a ribbon which used to be tied around its neck. Debbie dropped to her knees. "Poo Bear," she whispered as she picked up the pieces which once had been her teddy bear. She cradled the pieces to her chest.

Even though the door was slightly ajar, it was still closed enough to block any view of the bedroom. But in her mind's eye, Debbie could see as clearly as if the door was wide open.

He was there.

Sitting on her bed, his shoes soiling the bedspread.

Still clutching the pieces of Poo Bear, she slowly stood up. Feeling like a little girl, she dragged her feet as she continued to make her way toward the bedroom door. She pushed it open and a flood of emotions, ranging from sadness to resentment to hatred to bitterness, engulfed her like a giant spider's web.

The man on the bed glared at her, his eyes filled with venom.

Chapter 30

"And you're absolutely sure that there's no possible connection between the two envelopes," Dan said as he shoved the two handwriting examples into his shirt pocket. He was sitting in Richard's real estate office, a small room crowded with four desks. Each wall was occupied by charts listing property, which was either for sale or had just recently been sold.

"Very sure. Whoever wrote that first example was filled with lots of anger. This was missing from the second example." He took out a cigarette and lit it.

"Could it have been done by the same person, but the first time he was mad and the second time he wasn't?" Dan asked.

Richard shook his head. "Two different specimens."

Dan nodded. "Thanks, buddy." He pointed to the phone. "Mind if I use it?"

"Be my guest," he said, "and if you don't mind, those people over there are waiting for a closing. You don't need me anymore?"

Dan shook his head and waved. He dialed the police's number and asked to speak to Gilbert, their computer expert, but was informed that he wouldn't be back until tomorrow.

"I dropped a picture by earlier today. I was wondering if he's had a chance to work with it," Dan said.

"This is in reference to that picture where he's aging a lady?" a female officer asked.

"That's the one."

"I'm sorry, but no. But he did say that he'd have it by tomorrow."

Dan thanked her and hung up. As he started to walk out, he waved at Richard.

"Going home, you lucky crumb-bum?" Richard said when he saw Dan leaving.

"I wish. I still need to stop by the park and check on some stuff." Dan remembered his pen and returned to Richard's desk and retrieved it.

"Sounds like fun."

"Oh, yeah, loads. All I'd like to do is grab a hamburger, a cold beer, and hit the sack."

"Alone?"

"Not necessarily."

"I thought so. Call me when you find someone."

"Find your own," Dan said faking a frown.

* * *

Dan leaned back on the park bench and looked up at the trees. He'd been here for--he looked at his watch--over two hours, and all he found was exactly what he had expected to find: nothing. Not one damn bit of useful information.

Oh, he had learned a lot. From an old timer he discovered that the number of pigeons were diminishing each year. From a mother with three rowdy boys, he found out that she is the only mother who brings her kids to the park on a regular basis. All the other kids drag their maids. An old woman informed him that she no longer comes after sunset. There have been two rapes and one stabbing.

Dan sighed, stood up and headed toward his car. He

had already started the engine when an elderly lady pushing a grocery cart caught his attention. She was an old woman, bent and gnarled. Her dull, gray hair was pulled back in a loose bun. She wore a simple cotton dress which fit her like a parachute. Her cart was filled with small paper sack packages.

Dan turned the engine off and walked toward the old woman.

"Wanna buy some pigeon food, Mister?" She wiped her nose with her arm. "Only fifty cents. You get a big bag for the price."

Dan nodded as he reached into his pocket. He took out two quarters and handed them to her. "Do you come here often?"

"Everyday."

"Then you must know all of the regulars."

"Sure do and by name, too. Never forget a name or face." She smiled revealing a set of tobacco-stained teeth.

"Yeah?" Dan opened the package and threw some seeds on the ground. Immediately, the sidewalk became a moving mass of birds. "Wish I could be like that. But I always forget faces."

"Not me. Henry--that was my husband--he used to tell me, 'Gladys, you got yourself one of them photographic minds.' And I do."

Dan wondered if this bag lady was the reason why he was at the park. If so, he needed to find out who sent her--and why. He decided to test her boast and play her game. "Do you remember people you haven't seen in a long time?"

"Sure do."

"A friend of mine used to come here all the time." Dan threw more seeds down.

"Yeah? Who?"

"Oh, it was so long ago you probably don't know him--or remember him."

"Never forget a face, no matter how long, and I've been

coming here for 'bout ten years." She scratched her chin. "Bet I know him."

"Sam Capacini."

"He was your friend?" Her eyes narrowed with suspicion.

Dan smiled kindly at her. "Wasn't he everybody's friend?"

Slowly she nodded. "He was one hell of a good guy and he didn't kill nobody."

"There was a room full of people who said otherwise." He emptied the bag of seed.

"He pulled the trigger, Mister, but he didn't know what he was doing."

"Meaning?"

"Someone tricked him into doing it. Sam would never do nothing like that."

"Someone like who?"

The old woman shrugged. "Beats me." Then after a moment's pause she added, "Thought you said you was his friend. You'd know better than me."

"He never mentioned anything to me."

"Yeah, that's Sam all right." She threw her head back and let out a hearty laugh. "Never was much of a talker."

"No, I suppose not."

"That's why when that lady started coming and meeting with Sam on a daily basis, I was real surprised." She scratched her head and wrinkled her nose. "I never could figure out what they could be talkin' about."

"What lady was this?" Dan stared at the pigeons, hoping he didn't seem too anxious to gather information.

"Just a lady." She shrugged. "But I mean a *real* lady, with furs and diamonds."

"Wouldn't happen to know her name?" Dan shook the bag, freeing the few seeds still caught at the bottom of the sack. He watched the pigeons gather around his feet.

"I'm sure he mentioned it." She wrinkled her face. "Then again maybe not. I don't ever forget a name."

"Do you remember anything specific about her? Like the color of her hair, any distinguishing marks. Anything at all?"

"Hey! Are you a cop?"

"No, I'm not."

"Why you want to know all of this for?"

"Because I feel that we can clear up his name."

"How, if you're no cop?"

"I'm a reporter. I'll make sure the truth gets printed."

"Yeah?" She rubbed her chin and once again eyed him suspiciously. "You got one of them fancy press cards?"

Dan reached for his wallet and showed her the press card. "Help me to help him."

After a moment's hesitation, she said, "Okay. Like I says, he used to talk to this lady a lot. I betcha she'd be the one to talk to."

"I agree. But how do we get in touch with her?" Dan watched as the last pigeon flew away toward a group of young boys who were crumbling some bread and throwing it at them.

"I don't know her name, but I saw her picture in the paper once."

Dan immediately turned his attention to her. "When was this?"

"Two years." She scratched her throat as she looked up. "Maybe three."

"Which paper? Do you remember which page?"

"That's your car?" She pointed to a blue Chevy.

Dan nodded.

"Bet I could find it in the library." She eyed her cart filled with bags of pigeon food. "But I'd be losing customers and customers mean money."

"How much do you figure that cart is worth?" Dan asked.

She scratched the back of her head as she

contemplated the answer. "Ten. Maybe fifteen dollars."

Dan handed her a twenty dollar bill. "This says you come with me and show me that picture."

She smiled, a wide, toothy curvature of the lips. "Make it two of those and I'll go."

Reluctantly, Dan handed her another twenty.

Chapter 31

Debbie recognized the hatred in his eyes, but much to her surprise, the anguish she thought she would feel didn't come. Instead, she answered his venomous look with rising anger laced with bitterness, and yes, Debbie admitted, even a hatred of her own.

"What possible satisfaction did you get out of doing this to Poo Bear?" She shoved the pieces in front of him.

He smiled, a wide sadistic smile. "You loved that stupid stuffed bear, just like I loved your mother. You killed her, I killed your bear."

Debbie shook her head. She almost felt pity for him. "You're sick," she said. "You're really sick."

He answered her accusation with another evil-filled smile. And a memory flashed before her. She had recently seen this smile. She gasped. "That was you." Her mouth felt rough and dry. "Wasn't it? Out there by the lake? You--you tried to kill me."

"I could have, if I wanted to."

Feeling dizzy, Debbie took a step backwards. "What stopped you?"

"Let's just say that all of a sudden I remembered I was your father."

"My father!" She smirked and her eyes watered. *Damn me for being so weak.* She turned, giving him her back.

"You've never been my father. Where were you when I
needed you? Licking your wounds because Mom died." She
turned to face him, not caring if he did see her tears. "Do you
think I wanted her to die? I was a baby! I had nothing to do
with it, and I refuse to feel guilty anymore!"

Gunther bolted out of bed, his eyes pin points of anger.
"You bitch! You *are* guilty! You did kill her! You deserve to
die!"

His words--his tone--carved out a hollow pocket of fear
in Debbie's stomach. She felt her legs weaken. Afraid she
would plummet to the floor, her left arm reached for the
dresser and held on to its top. For a second, her eyes traveled
to the top of her dresser. She spotted a brush and a metal rat-
tail comb. She could, if need be, use those as weapons.

Debbie turned her eyes toward her father. His fists
were clenched, his jaw taut with anger. Better calm him down.
"Daddy." She sounded like a two year old. "Mom wouldn't
want to see us fighting. What can I do to make up for lost
time?"

Within measurable seconds, the fury in his face was
replaced by a vacant look. Gradually, his features softened,
but his eyes held the warmth of an ice cube. "Pay me."

Involuntary, tremors ignited within Debbie. "What?"

"Out there by the lake. I could've killed you. You know
that." His voice no longer rang with anger. Instead, his tone
was very matter-of-fact.

And somehow Debbie found this to be more frightening
than his anger. She felt clammy wet fear crawl across her
skin.

"I was going to kill you," he continued in the same
nonchalant way. "Then I changed my mind. You are worth a
lot more to me alive than dead."

Debbie breathed a little easier. At least for the moment,
she was safe. But still she stood perfectly still, afraid any
movement or comment would turn him once again into a

violent, irrational creature.

"Do you know how I got in?" He took a step toward her.

Debbie willed herself to remain perfectly still even though her mind shouted at her to run. She shook her head.

"I told the security guard that I was your old man. He said the resemblance was strong. I was going to show him my driver's license, but he said he didn't need it. He knew I was telling the truth." He extended his index finger and roughly ran it underneath Debbie's chin. "See how easy it is to see you, *daughter?*" He laughed contemptuously and walked toward the bedroom door.

Debbie relaxed a bit more.

"Now I figure I can get hold of your boyfriend and tell him all about your childhood. I'll begin by telling him how you were a wall-flower, a Plain Jane. It wasn't until you started imitating this Colette that you became a someone. I'll show the world what Deborah Ann Gunther really is: a big, fat nothing. Take Colette away from you, and you don't even amount to a pile of shit." He leaned on the door frame. "I'm sure your fans would love to find out that their heroine is a big fake." He crossed his arms in front of him and smiled sweetly. There almost was an unnerving charm about him. "Are you interested in finding out how I can keep quiet?"

Debbie thought that he was a fool but nevertheless nodded one time signifying yes.

"I would say twenty thousand dollars would do for openers."

Debbie felt as if an arrow hit her just below the heart. Automatically, she turned, opened the top drawer and took out the checkbook.

In the wink of an eye, he was upon her. He slapped her so hard, the impact sent her sprawling to the floor.

"Bitch!" he yelled. "Do you think I'm stupid or something?" His body shook with anger.

"What...I..."

"You were going to write me a check? Why? So that as soon as I walk out of here, you put a stop payment on it? You must think I'm a total idiot." He raised his arm to hit her again.

Debbie protectively raised her arms in front of her. "I don't have that kind of cash in the room. The only way to get it is to bring the security men up here. I thought you wouldn't want that. Besides, I wasn't going to put a stop payment."

He backed away. "Security, huh? Why?"

"My money is in the downstairs safe. I can request it, but security will have to bring it up."

He thought about it for a moment. "Do it."

"I'll do it all right," she said, standing up. "But in return, I don't ever want to see you again. You can talk to whichever reporters you please and tell them whatever you please. But anything you tell will only make you look stupid. It'll only show them what an ugly man you really are."

She picked up the phone and requested the cash. When she finished, she slammed the phone down and stared at her father. "From now on, if you so much as step one foot in the same city I'm in, I'll press charges. Remember, you tried to kill me and I have a witness. Spend the money any way you want, but I don't ever want to see you again!"

He looked her over and held her at bay with his large, brown, evaluating eyes. Slowly, he smiled. "You're finally showing some guts. Too bad it came so late. I might have learned to accept you." He stared at her intently, and she stared back him.

A knock on the door interrupted them. "Who is it?" Debbie asked.

"Security."

Debbie opened the door, accepted the cash, and signed for it. She thanked the two men who brought it up and tipped them five dollars each.

Turning to her father, she said, "Take it and get out!"

He smirked, grabbed the money and hissed, "Good-bye,

daughter."

Debbie slammed the door shut, rubbed her eyes, cleared her throat, and headed for the bedroom.

She saw the remains of Poo Bear laying on the bed. An overwhelming sense of loss struck her and drained her soul. She reached for the teddy bear. "Poo Bear. Poo Bear, you're gone. Gone." She buried her face in what once was the teddy bear's chest. "Damn you!" She raised her head. "I won't give in to you! I won't. I WON'T!"

* * *

Debbie stared at her face in the mirror. She had tried to be strong, but the memory of her father gnawed at her like a giant insect. Her face was creased with sorrow. "It's no good, Annie," she said. "If Jack saw me like this he'd fire me instantly. I don't look much like Colette now, do I?"

Alarm opened Annie's eyes extra wide. "What are you saying, child? You're gonna quit?"

Had she not felt like screaming inside, Debbie would have laughed. Instead, she just smirked. "No, Annie, nothing like that." She walked away from the mirror and sat beside Annie on her bed. "It's my da--father."

"Oh?"

"He...he's always...hated me." Debbie choked on the word *hate*. "I tried to make him love me, but--" She shook herself. "Anyway, he just left a few minutes ago. That's why I called you. I had to talk to someone."

"I'm here for you, child." She reached out and wrapped her hands around Debbie's.

"He tried to kill me, Annie. He was the one out there by the lake."

"Him?" There was stunned disbelief on Annie's face. "Not Jack Armstrong?"

Debbie shook her head. "I saw him, Annie, but I didn't want to accept it. That's why I couldn't remember." A shuddering spasm racked her body. "All of this time, it was him. He was the one who wrote that note and called me in the middle of the night. He was responsible for the firecrackers and the dress and flowers."

"No!" Annie bolted out of bed.

"Annie, what's wrong?" Surprise momentarily pushed Debbie's sorrow away.

"He couldn't have!"

"What are you talking about?"

"He might have done all those other things, but I swear child, that man had nothin' to do with the dress and flowers."

"He had to, Annie. Both of those things were charged to my account. I found him in my bedroom. Who knows how many more times he had come in snooping through my items until he found my VISA card?"

"No, no, no! That's not how it works."

"I don't understand, Annie. What are you trying to say?"

"I don't know." She started to pace, her arms fluttering like bird wings. "I don't know. I got to think. It's not supposed to work like this."

"What's not supposed to work like this?" Debbie stood up and blocked Annie so that now they faced each other.

"What about that note Colette wrote to you?" Annie crossed her arms in front of her.

"Annie, I talked to Dan about that letter. He said he followed the investigation very carefully. He swears Sam Capacini acted alone when he killed Colette."

"No! That's not true."

"Annie, level with me. What do you know about this?"

"Nothing, child. All I know is that I was sure you were going to help me find Colette's real killer, but now it seems that's not going to happen."

"Why is this so important to you, Annie?"

"I like to keep my promises. I promised Colette that I would help her."

"Dan told me that after Colette died, there were rumors

that Sam Capacini was part of a conspiracy. Was that your doing?"

Annie nodded. "Yes, I did that, but people laughed at me. That's why I stopped doing it, and I've felt plenty bad about that. I thought since your life was in danger, you'd want to find the real killer."

"Oh, Annie, it's over now. All of this time it was my father. It had nothing to do with Colette. We were wrong. Can't you see that?"

"I say we weren't wrong. This isn't over. Not by a long shot." She turned and stormed out of the door, leaving a confused Debbie behind.

Chapter 32

Debbie ran to the phone and dialed Dan's number. *Please pick it up.* Half of her almost wished that Sexy Voice would answer so that Debbie could leave a message. The other half was praying Sexy Voice wouldn't be there.

When no one answered the phone, she slammed it down, her hand resting on the cradle, her heart thumping so wildly she could feel it in her ears.

Someone knocked on the door.

What now?

The knocking persisted as though urgently insisting that Debbie open the door. "Who is it?" she asked through the closed door.

"It's me, Bill."

Debbie recalled Dan's warning: stay away from him until you hear from me. But her father had written that note. The danger was gone. She swung the door open.

"I was wondering if we could talk," Bill said softly. He looked around the hallway, shuffled his feet, and cleared his throat. He looked as comfortable as a reindeer in a den of lions. "May I come in?" he finally asked.

Debbie stepped aside, allowing him to enter. She left the front door wide open. "May I offer you a drink?" she asked.

Bill shook his head. When he noticed that the front door

was open, he smiled. "I'm afraid you have the wrong impression of me," he said.

Debbie chose to ignore his comment and instead asked, "Did something go wrong with the show?"

Bill shook his head, stared at Debbie for a considerable amount of time then asked, "Did you know that Colette and I were planning to get married?"

"I had heard a rumor to that effect."

"It was no rumor, Debbie." A vacant, sick look covered his eyes. "I loved Colette like I have never loved anyone. That's why, when Jack suggested bringing in a Colette impersonator, I was upset. I didn't think I could handle it. And that's why I decided to put the make on you--to discourage you and to see just how far you would go."

"Did I pass your test?" Debbie was aware that her tone was laced with sarcasm.

Bill seemed oblivious to it. "With flying colors," he answered, "and that's why I'm going to stick my neck way out. It may cost me my job and very easily my life, but I want to warn you about Jack Armstrong."

Debbie felt an icy tentacle of apprehension wrap around her. "Please sit down," she said. "I'll close the door."

After Debbie had settled down on the plush arm chair opposite Bill, he began to speak. "There is a multi-millionaire who has two weaknesses, and one of them is gambling. His name is Harry Watkins. Have you met him?"

"Jack pointed him out to me during the publicity supper. What's his second weakness?"

"Colette."

"Yeah, so?"

"So that means that he has an almost perverted love for Colette. When Colette was..." A distant, hollow look glazed his eyes. He swallowed hard. "...murdered, he blamed the casino. Naturally, it wasn't the casino's fault, but he stopped coming anyway. I heard he started taking his business to

Atlantic City."

For a moment, Bill remained silent. The way that his eyes sparkled, then almost immediately turned void, Debbie knew he was remembering Colette. He sighed, then continued, "Jack is a very power-hungry man and has been as long as I can remember. When Mr. Lovingsworth first started getting sick, Jack began scheming to get ahead. That obviously worked, because he's almost in the number two position. All he has to do is beat his main competition, a man by the name of Thomas Buller."

"How does he plan to do this?"

"By bringing back that one big account."

"And that's this...uh, Harry, uh--"

"Watkins. Harry Watkins. Yes, that's where he comes in."

Debbie nodded. "All right. I can understand that. But why are you telling me this?"

"Because this is where you step into the picture. Harry was--or I should say, is--so obsessed with Colette that Jack specifically hired you as a lure to bring Harry's money back to the Crystal Palace Casino."

Debbie's throat tightened. "You mean there's going to be no show?"

"I didn't say that. The Colette show is part of the lure."

"What about Hollywood and New York?"

Bill shook his head. "There is no Hollywood or New York for you. But there will be an After Opening Night Party where you will meet Harry."

"What will happen then?"

Bill smiled a dry smile. "Not much, I'm afraid. You will either marry Harry, become his mistress or continue to be one of the hundreds of struggling Colette impersonators. In other words, Debbie, Jack hired you to become nothing more than a high-paid hooker."

Debbie's mind was too numbed to make sense of any

of this information.

"There's one more thing," Bill said.

Debbie stared at him.

"Regardless of Jack's plans for you, I plan to continue with the show. I would like for you to come to tonight's eight o'clock performance where the Crystalites will honor you as their special guest. Then you can personally invite the audience to your own opening night. We're going to make this a successful show, in spite of Jack's plans."

* * *

The Boss stood by the base of the fountain outside the Crystal Palace Casino staring at the life-sized statues of the children as they threw water up in the air. The angle from which the lights hit the water made it seem as though they were throwing crystals. It was beautiful. In fact, the entire casino was absolutely beautiful, but there was an ugliness inside.

That ugliness was Debbie Gunther.

She knew too much about Colette's death. Of this, the Boss was sure. But the Boss's main concern was finding out how she knew so much.

The Boss could have ordered Debbie's death a long time ago, but had decided to wait, hoping to learn the source. But this was no longer practical.

The only way to protect the secret of Colette's murder was to get rid of Debbie along with everyone else who might be supplying Debbie with that information.

That many deaths would require a lot of careful planning, but it could be done. After all, hadn't the Boss already gotten away with one perfect murder?

Very soon, the Boss decided, the deaths would start.

* * *

Dan didn't like it one bit. Information seldom came this easily. He was being set up, but by the person who wanted Debbie dead or by the person who wanted Debbie to find

Colette's murderer? Or were they the same person? A feeling of uneasiness crept over Dan's body.

He stopped at a stop sign and took the opportunity to glance at Gladys. Was she who she claimed to be: a bag lady or a darn good actress? "Who are you?"

The question seemed to startle Gladys and she shook herself. "What do you mean by that? You know who I am. I'm Gladys."

"So you say." Dan was forced to slow down when a car cut in front of him. "Finding you in the park like I did was too much of a coincidence, and I'm not one to believe in coincidences."

Gladys visibly tensed. "Look, Mister, just 'cuz I'm nice, I'm doing this for you. But I'm not going to put up with you questioning me. You say you don't know who I am, well, I don't know who you are. Maybe all you plan to do is take me to a cheap motel and rape me. If you're gonna question me, then I want out now."

Dan exhaled slowly. "Sorry," he said, "it's just that a person who is very important to me is being threatened. Somebody wants her dead, and it might have something to do with finding out who set up Sam Capacini."

Gladys frowned. "You said your friend is being threatened?"

Dan nodded.

"Look, Mister, I had no idea somebody was playing games like this."

"Does that mean that somebody paid you to show up at the park and tell me this story?"

"I sell pigeon food at the park. I've been doing that for 'bout ten years. I told you this before." She folded her arms in front of her.

"So you went there to sell your little bags and not to talk to me."

Gladys remained quiet and fixed her eyes directly in

front of her.

Dan slowed down so he could reach for his wallet. He produced a ten-dollar bill and showed it to Gladys. "Now, do you remember?"

"Nope. It was a twenty last time."

Dan glared at her. "Well, it's a ten this time. Now tell me, did someone send you to talk to me?"

"Look, Mister, I'm here as a favor to you. I'm gonna help ya find that broad who'd talk to Sam Capacini all of the time. That's the one you want. Nothing else matters."

Dan stuffed the ten into his shirt pocket. From the side of his eyes, he glanced at Gladys. She was protecting someone. He wondered who.

* * *

Alarm pinched Gladys' face. "Hey, Mister. This isn't the way to the library," Gladys said when Dan took a different exit than the one she was expecting him to.

"We're making a small detour," Dan said. "We're going to the police station."

"Hey! I don't know nothing else than what I told you. I swear--"

"Relax, Gladys. I just want to catch a guy before he leaves. He has some pictures for me."

"Can I wait here in the car for you?"

"Will you take off?"

"Where could I go? You are my ride back to my side of town."

Dan nodded, turned off the engine, and put the keys in his pocket. "I'll be back in less than five minutes," he said as he slammed the door shut and ran up the stairs.

Detective Ronnie Higgins was coming out just as Dan was ready to enter the building. "Back again? Dan, you were here only two days ago. I told you, if I find anything--"

"Relax, Ronnie, I'm not here about Diana. I'm here to see Gilbert."

Ronnie smiled, obviously relieved. "Don't get me wrong. I'm still looking for your daughter, but the trail is cold."

"I know." A stabbing pain hit Dan deep in the heart. "But I'll never give up."

Ronnie nodded. "Gilbert is still in there. But you better hurry. He's getting ready to leave."

Dan thanked him and hurried inside. He found Gilbert stuffing some papers into a briefcase. When he saw Dan approaching, he opened his drawer and retrieved a folder. He handed it to Dan.

"Gilbert, thanks so much for doing that picture on such short notice."

Gilbert smiled. "That's okay, but I'd say we're even now. This is my way of saying thanks for all the P.R. you've given the police department."

Dan reached for the folder. "Okay, so we're even." He looked at the thick folder. "Why so many?"

"I made several versions of what she probably looks like now. You know, it gives you more choices. Does she have something to do with your daughter's disappearance?"

"No. It's for a story I'm writing. You remember, I told you about it. It involves Debbie." He opened the file and studied the picture on top. He recognized her. She looked vaguely familiar, but something wasn't right. Dan frowned and moved on to the second picture.

This one was way off. Way too fat. He was looking or someone slimmer. Perhaps a bit younger too. He set the picture down. He glanced at the third picture and froze.

"You know her," Gilbert said.

Dan nodded. "It's Annie," he answered.

"Annie?"

"She's Debbie's personal maid and also used to be Colette's personal maid."

"And?"

"And I think she was also Mr. Lovingsworth's mistress."

"Oh, oh. What does that mean?"

Dan paused for a while, sorting out the information. "It means that Annie's daughter is Ms. Elizabeth's sister, and that's how Annie knew that Ms. Elizabeth had found a 'fake' sister."

"So who's Annie's daughter?"

Dan shook his head. "I don't know, but I intend to find out." He thought about it, remembering the other day. He and Debbie had speculated whether or not Annie had drugged the juice. He had told Debbie he'd check on that, but dammit, he hadn't followed through.

He had screwed up again. If anything happened to Debbie because of his stupidity...

He reached for the phone. "Gil, I need to use this." He dialed Debbie's number as fast as he could.

With growing apprehension, he let the phone ring for quite a while. "Answer it!" he ordered under his breath. "Answer the damn phone." But no matter how long he let it ring, he knew Debbie wasn't going to answer.

Dan slammed the phone down and ran back to the car.

Chapter 33

Debbie stared at the pitcher of juice. She wondered, again, if Annie had drugged her. Then she remembered that it had been Annie who had given her Colette's letter. Debbie, like a fool, had accepted Annie's word that Colette had written that letter.

Maybe Debbie should question Annie--especially since Annie had reacted so strangely when Debbie told her that no one, after all, was after her. It had all been her father's doing. Yet, Annie insisted that it wasn't solely her father.

Debbie chewed on her lip and got the sudden urge to talk to Annie. She had Annie paged. While she waited to hear from Annie, Debbie picked up a copy of the newspaper. She read the same paragraph several times, but still she couldn't concentrate on it. She set the paper down and paged Annie again.

The soft female voice over the phone said, "I'm sorry, Ms. Gunther, but Annie isn't answering her page. Maybe she went home early. She's definitely not here in the casino."

Debbie thanked her and was about to call Annie when the phone began to ring. She picked up the phone on the first ring.

"Miss Gunther? This is Marie at make-up. I've been

expecting you."

Debbie hit her forehead. "Marie! I'm sorry. I forgot to call and cancel."

"Does that mean you won't be needing me at all?"

"Not tonight, Marie. But please cover for me. I'll put the make-up on myself, but if anybody asks you, please tell them you did it."

"Would I get in trouble for that? What if it's not done right and Bill or Jack comes and chews my ass out?"

"Then I'll tell them the truth. But I assure you, nobody is going to chew you out."

There was a sigh followed by a meek, "Okay. But why are you doing this?"

"Marie, I have a problem that I need to work out. If I can't do that, I won't be able to concentrate tonight, and my impersonation won't be that good. I figured if I put the make-up on myself, I'd have twenty minutes to spare. I could use that extra time to work my problem out."

"If you feel that's necessary," Marie said, "that's fine with me. Whatever your problem is, Miss Gunther, I hope you solve it. If you don't mind me saying so, you sound terrible."

Debbie glanced up and looked at herself in the mirror. Her eyes, in spite of the make-up, drooped and lacked the spark which Colette had been famous for. Her features, in general, sagged. Her contact with her father had affected her more deeply than she wanted to admit. "I'll be okay," she said. "Thanks for your concern."

She hung up the phone and was about to dial Annie's number when there came a knock at her door. "I'm glad you're here," Bill Davis said. "I know it's still early, but I wanted--hey, are you all right?"

Debbie nodded.

"Are you sure? You look like the world has deserted you. That won't do at all. Whatever's eating you, you've got to cover it up. That's what actresses do."

Debbie forced a smile.

"That's better," Bill said. "Now keep that smile and pretend you're happy. I want us to walk through the casino. I got a few photographers waiting. That should generate a bit of enthusiasm. It'll be good for the show."

"Bill, couldn't I make a phone call first?"

"No time now," Bill said as he grabbed her arm and pulled her along. "Now don't forget to do your Colette stuff."

Debbie nodded and promised herself that even if she had to sneak away from Bill, she would contact Annie tonight.

* * *

As soon as Dan and Gladys reached the library, Dan dashed toward the public phone. He dialed Debbie's number. He let the phone ring for a long time before hanging up. He stood staring at the phone, anxiety gnawing at him until he felt like a trapped stallion in a burning stable.

Dammit! If only Debbie would answer the phone, he'd know she was safe, and he'd be able to concentrate on his research.

He dropped another quarter in the telephone slot and dialed the casino's number where he asked to be connected to Bill Davis' office.

"I'm sorry, but Mr. Davis is out right now. May I help you?"

"Yes, this is Dan Springer, and I'm working against a deadline. It's very urgent that I speak to Ms. Debbie Gunther as soon as possible. Do you know how I can reach her?"

"Just a minute, please."

Dan heard the clicking of the line signifying he was being put on hold. Soft music replaced the silence. A few moments later, Dan heard the receiver being picked up again.

"If you want me to," came the same voice over the phone, "I can leave a message for Ms. Gunther to call you as soon as she's available, but that won't be for several hours. She's scheduled to attend the eight o'clock show where she will be introduced to the audience. Bill anticipates that after the show, a group will gather around Debbie, and he isn't really sure at exactly what time Debbie can get back with you. Is there anything he can help you with?"

"No, thank you. Just please tell Debbie to call me as soon as possible. I can work my deadline around her schedule." Dan hung up and let out a sigh of relief. Debbie was probably in make-up right now, then she'd be busy with the show and fans. She should be safe for several hours. That meant that he could now spend his time getting the answers he needed to complete the puzzle.

Walking briskly, he headed toward the microfilm section where he had left Gladys with the tedious job of finding the picture.

"Any luck?" he asked.

Gladys shook her head.

Dan sighed, and he too began searching the microfilm. Because of Gladys' prior description, Dan had a good idea of what he was looking for. Consequently, anytime he came to a picture which remotely resembled the one Gladys had described, he would call her over.

Each time she shook her head, returned to her own machine, and continued her search. With each passing minute, Dan's stomach burned a bit more until he felt as if he had swallowed live coal. Who was this mysterious woman who had befriended Sam?

On page three-B, a woman with a plastered smile stared back at him. She was shaking hands with a man not quite as tall as she. "Is this it?" he asked. He held his breath in anticipation.

Gladys rolled her chair toward him, glanced at it, shook her head, and returned her attention to her own machine. She withdrew the microfilm reel she had just finished and inserted a new one.

Dan watched her for a minute, then turned his attention to his own machine. A few minutes later, he heard Gladys gasp.

He looked up at her. She was leaning over, her eyes narrow slits in her face. She tapped the screen, pointing to a picture.

Dan wished she would say something. He felt his anxiety grow, causing him to grimace. Unable to wait any longer, he asked, "Did you find it?"

Gladys ignored him and continued to study the picture. Her head bopped.

"Gladys, did you find it?"

She looked up at Dan and while still seated, pushed her chair away from the machine. "Yep. That's her. I swear to it!"

Dan felt his heart catch in his throat as he stood up to look at the picture.

Chapter 34

Bill escorted Debbie inside the showroom and led her to the very front seat, right by the center stage.

"Hey, Debbie!" someone called as they walked past a table.

Debbie turned, smiled, winked, and kept on going.

"You're a big hit," Bill whispered in her ear. "Most people don't remember impersonators' names. But they remember you. You were absolutely fantastic out there."

Debbie wrinkled her nose and sat down. Someone snapped her picture just as the lights dimmed. The dancers came out and did a modernized version of "Raindrops."

Someone tapped Debbie and asked for her autograph. She signed it and noticed that the main star, a well-known entertainer by the name of Stephanie Lane, gave her a brief, but very dirty look. Debbie signed the autograph, thanked the person and walked out.

Bill caught her outside and grabbed her by the arm. "What do you think you're doing?"

"Bill!" She turned, startled. "Stephanie was giving me the eye. I was getting the attention instead of her. I thought I'd wait out here."

"She's going to call you up on stage."

"But that won't be until the end of the show. I'll be there fifteen minutes before it's over."

Bill nodded. "Okay, and thanks for putting up with

Stephanie. She's got a vile temper and an ego the size of Texas." He went back inside.

Debbie nodded and headed directly toward the public phones by the casino's check-in counter. She looked up Annie's number and dialed. "Hi," she said once she heard a *Hello.* "I'm calling from the Crystal Palace Casino, and I'd like to talk to Annie."

"I'm sorry, she's not here," came the female voice over the phone, "but I'm Sue Lynn Kapetzy, Annie's roommate. Can I help you?"

"No, I don't think so. I need to talk to Annie. Do you know how I can reach her?"

"She's not at work? That's where she's suppose to be. If she isn't there, I have no idea where she'd be. Have you checked the casino for her?"

"Yes, I did, but either she's ignoring my page, or she's not here."

"That's very unusual. If she plans to go someplace other than work, she always lets me know."

"In that case, I'm sure she's here someplace. I just missed her for some reason."

"I'll tell her to call you as soon as she can."

"Please do." Debbie hung the phone and headed toward the main casino. She stopped to watch an elderly woman who had just won a recreational vehicle by dropping three-dollars in the slot machine.

"Excuse me, aren't you Colette?"

Debbie turned, remembering to smile. "I impersonate Colette. Are you coming to my show?"

"You bet!" said the slightly over-weight lady. "I wasn't sure if it was you. You look like her, but you look so--so worried. Are you okay?"

"Yes, of course," Debbie lied. "Thanks for your concern. I'll see you in the audience."

"Yeah, sure."

Debbie headed straight for the casino's bathroom. Its entrance made Debbie feel she was entering a queen's chamber. There was a large sitting room, its walls covered with mirrors. On top of the polished marble counters rested three boxes of Kleenex, two bottles of perfumes, and several crystal ash trays.

Debbie stared at herself in the mirror. This wouldn't do at all. She must put on a happy mask and erase those worry frowns. She did a quick make-up repair job while two teenagers watched and attempted to imitate her.

By the time Debbie returned to the show, it was more than half-over. Instead of going to her seat, she chose to stand by the door. This way she wouldn't rob Stephanie of any attention.

During the last five minutes of the show, Stephanie invited Debbie to come up on stage. Immediately, the room filled with thunderous applause. Stephanie kissed Debbie on the cheek. "She's great, folks. Wait until you catch her show. You'll love it." She raised Debbie's hand in triumph.

The audience clapped and cheered louder. "Opening night is in three days," Debbie said. "You're all invited."

The curtain slowly began to descend. Stephanie held onto Debbie's hand and both bowed and threw kisses to the audience. Just as soon as the curtains touched the floor, Stephanie dropped Debbie's hand and snapped, "You bitch. You purposely stole my show. I don't ever want you to come back." She stormed off before Debbie could answer.

Bill immediately grabbed the stunned Debbie and took her out to mingle with the crowd.

* * *

"If I can talk Stephanie into letting us introduce you in her show again, I'd like to do it at least one more time before opening night," Bill told Debbie. "Maybe even for tonight's midnight performance." They were sitting in his cramped office, opening up some boxes of publicity pictures.

"I don't know, Bill. Stephanie was really upset," Debbie answered.

"You leave Stephanie to me. It's you I'm worried about."

"Oh?"

"Now don't get me wrong. You were great tonight. But you weren't all there. Your mind was elsewhere, and we can't have that. So I'll tell you what we're going to do. I'll give you an hour off. Use it to take care of whatever is bothering you. Then, when that hour is over, you're mine again. That means that you'll be at your best with not a trace of problems showing. Fair enough?"

Debbie nodded, thanked him, and hurried out. An hour would be ample time to find Annie.

* * *

"I gather you recognize the lady in the picture," Gladys said. The lady using the microfilm machine next to her gave her a dirty look for talking so loudly. "Well, did ya?" she whispered.

Numbly, Dan nodded. "That's the 'Boss who sits up there and rules everyone,' the owner of the Crystal Palace Casino, Ms. Elizabeth Lovingsworth herself." He kept his voice low.

Gladys stared at Dan through wide, unblinking eyes. "Are you saying that the owner of the Crystal Palace Casino is the one who met with Sam Capacini every day? But why?"

Dan's mind spun with unanswered questions. "I don't know. You tell me." He sat down and rolled his chair next to Gladys'.

"Me? Why me? You're the hot-shot reporter." She dabbed her mouth with her hand.

"You were there, Gladys. What did Ms. Elizabeth and Sam talk about?"

Gladys' eyes pinched together, giving her a wary, hawk-like look. "I never listen to other people's conversations. I mind my own business."

Dan reached into his wallet and produced another twenty. He waved it in front of her. "This bill is yours if you tell me what you know."

Gladys moved her lips as though chewing on something. "I told you. I don't listen to other people talk."

Dan shrugged and began to replace the bill in his wallet.

"Wait!" Gladys leaned a bit toward him. "Now, it ain't much. Like I says: I really don't like to eavesdrop. But one time I noticed Sam was real excited. I mean I never seen him like that.

"Anyways, he shouts the word 'Colette' and he starts waving his arms up and down. That fancy lady immediately hushes him, but Sam shouted the word so loud, I couldn't help but hear." Before Dan had a chance to react, she snatched the twenty out of his hand. "I figured I earned this, 'cuz I told you all I know."

"That's not exactly true, Gladys."

Gladys stiffened. "What do you mean? I did tell you everything I know."

"You didn't tell me how you happened to be in the park today."

"I sell pigeon food."

"And you just happened to go there when I was there."

"That's right."

"And you just happened to remember Sam Capacini."

"That's also right."

"And you just happened to remember that Ms. Elizabeth used to come talk to Sam Capacini."

"Didn't know who she was until today."

"But you did remember her picture appeared in a newspaper which is five years old."

"I did. I got me one of those photographic memories. Remember?"

"Yes, I remember." Dan stood up and placed himself

behind her. Gladys' eyes followed him, but he gently moved her face forward. "Just keep looking straight ahead, Gladys, and describe me."

"Describe you?"

"Yeah, describe me. How tall am I? What color are my eyes? What am I wearing?"

"Well, I uh--"

"You can't remember, can you?"

"Maybe I remember only the people I want to remember. Maybe I don't want to remember you."

"Or maybe you can't remember more than the average person does." He walked around and sat beside her. "Gladys, I don't know if you understand the gravity of this situation, but a young, innocent woman can die because of these games you're playing. If that happens, then you're an accessory to murder."

Gladys' eyes popped open in alarm. "Murder? I feed pigeons, mister. How could I possibly get involved in a murder?"

"By withholding information. If you don't tell me how you knew I was going to show up, and how you just happened to remember all of this information, then something might happen to Debbie. If it does, then I'm coming back with a vengeance. If need be, I'll take you to the police, and they'll make you talk."

Gladys gasped. "Okay, okay. You win. All I know is that this lady paid me to lead you to that newspaper article." She spoke quickly. Her finger folded and unfolded several times in a nervous gesture.

"How did this lady know I was coming?"

"She said she put a note by Debbie's door, right where she was sure to find it."

"You know Debbie?"

"No, but she's suppose to look like Colette. She wouldn't have been hard to recognize."

"But she didn't show up."

"Nope, you did instead. This lady called back later and told me maybe Debbie might not come. Maybe you would. She described you pretty good."

"Who was this lady?"

Gladys shrugged. "Just a lady. I never met her before. She just sort of showed up one day but one thing I want you to know. I knew Sam. I wasn't lying about that. I liked him, and I never believed he was really guilty. He was a sweet, gullible kid. Somehow he was tricked, and I want to clear his name. That's why when this lady came and told me what she planned to do--and offered to pay me for it--I agreed."

"What did she look like? Did she give you a name?"

"Nope, didn't need to. She doesn't know this, but I recognized her."

"Oh?"

"She always hung around Colette. Every time someone snapped Colette's picture, there she was in the background. They said she was Colette's personal maid, but me, I never believed that."

"What do you mean?"

Gladys eyed him sharply. "Any fool could tell she was more than just her maid."

"Meaning?"

Gladys sniffled and shrugged. "Dunno, mister. I was just passing on gossip."

Chapter 35

Dan remembered when newspaper morgues used to be small, hot dingy rooms, but like everything else today, they too had gone modern and computerized. Consequently, it only took Dan a few seconds to punch up the program on a computer terminal and order it to search through the years of news and call up every story ever written about Colette.

Unfortunately, this was as far as the computer could help. What he was looking for--Colette's real name and/or her parents' names--could only be found by skimming each story.

After going through several articles, Dan rubbed his eyes. He was tired, and the words seemed to be running together. If only it wasn't so late at night, he could get the information easier elsewhere, but at this time of the night this was all he could think of. He wiped the sweat from his brow and continued with his search.

The next article--the hundredth, he felt--was titled "Colette: A Goddess." On the second paragraph he found the information he was looking for. "Finally!" he muttered under his breath. He reached for his pocket notebook and pencil and jotted down the following information:

> Colette:
> Baptized Jo Ann L. Basin
> No explanation given for the *L*
> Born May 26, 1976
> Boulder City, Nevada

He stared at the words for a while, studying and analyzing them. Colette's middle name had been L. L like in *Lovingsworth?*

Stuart Lovingsworth had had a mistress--someone he was apparently ashamed to have. Someone like a maid? Someone like Annie? The more he thought about it, the more he was convinced that was the case.

What he needed was more information on Colette's family background. And he knew exactly where to get it. Dan flipped the pages of his notebook until he found the phone number he was looking for: Stanley Bales'. He was a V.I.P. at City Records and he owed Dan a favor.

The phone rang fifteen times before a very sleepy, slurry voice snarled, "Hello?"

"Stan, this is Dan Springer."

"My God, man, do you know what time it is?"

"Well, it's not two in the morning," Dan answered.

There was a small pause, then: "I suppose that's the time I called you."

"Yep."

"And I suppose you want me to pay you back for withholding that information until I announced my candidacy for political office."

"Yep."

"I knew I had to pay you back sometime. And I guess now is the time, so go ahead and shoot."

"I need to verify the name of Colette's mother."

"That's it? You call me past ten just to find out the name of Colette's mother? My God, man, can't--"

"Stan, it's urgent. I think that a woman by the name of Annie is Colette's mother. If so, that would make Colette Ms. Elizabeth's real half-sister."

"Come on, Dan, there's more. Tell me the rest."

Dan hesitated. "Debbie Gunther is working for the Crystal Palace Casino. She impersonates Colette, and , as you might recall, that's the same casino Colette was killed in."

"Okay, so?"

"So Debbie and I, well, I think someone wants her dead, and I'm sure it has something to do with Colette's murder."

"Gee, Dan, this is heavy stuff. But are you sure you can't wait until tomorrow? I mean, the poor girl died five years ago. Surely, a few more hours can't hurt."

"It's not that simple, Stan. If I'm right, Debbie could be in a lot of danger right this moment."

There was a short pause, then: "All right, you convinced me. What do you want me to do?"

"One, keep this information to yourself."

"Hey, who would I tell?"

"I know you owe lots of reporters favors. We don't call you Stan the Man for nothing. Remember, this is my story and if there's a leak, I'll know where it came from."

"Okay, so I'm silent. What else do you want?"

"I want to look at Colette's birth certificate."

There were a few seconds of silence, then Stan the Man sighed and said, "Meet me in the my office in half-an-hour."

"You got it." Dan slammed the phone down and as he ran to his car, he fished the keys out of his pocket. The growing terror within him fueled him and filled him with dread.

Dan was depending on the show and publicity get-together afterwards to keep Debbie safe for the next couple of hours. By attending these functions, that should keep her away from both Ms. Elizabeth and Annie. By the time he got all of his information, he'd be there for Debbie.

And she'd be safe.

Chapter 36

Debbie returned to her suite and double-locked the door behind her. She fought off the urge to check the bathroom, beneath the bed, inside the closet, behind the curtains, the balcony. Why was she being paranoid?

Because she didn't feel safe.

Why? Because she had no one to trust.

She reached for the top shelf in her closet and brought down the shoe box. She found what was left of Poo Bear and underneath it, a photo.

Mom and Dad. Before she came along and ruined it for them. Her parents were so happy back then. And now Mom was dead. She could still hear her father's words cutting through the air like an ice knife. *She died giving birth to you. She could have saved herself, but she chose not to. Why did you have to kill her?*

Debbie took the picture to the bed and gently set it down on the night stand. *Mom, I'm sorry. I didn't want you to die.* She sat down and drew her knees up beneath her chin, wrapping her arms around her legs. She rocked back and forth, trying to control her feelings.

Mom, something happened. I met a man who can't love me. I had a friend I thought I could trust. She might have drugged me, Mom. I don't know if she drugged me, Mom. I don't know if she did.

Mom, I thought I had a career. But I don't. I was just being used to bring back a big account. I was hired as a whore.

And Mom, Dad came today. He tried to kill me, Mom. My own father tried to kill me.

What is wrong with me, Mom?

And why did I have to kill you?

She picked up the picture and stared at it. There were things in her childhood, she realized, that she had no control over. Things that would always be part of her.

But there were also things she could change. She unfolded and reached for the phone.

First, she dialed Dan's home phone. When there was no answer, she tried his office.

"Sorry, Debbie, I have no idea where he is, but I'll be glad to tell him you called," Dan's editor said.

Debbie thanked him and hung up. She tried Annie's house. No, she still hadn't arrived.

She remembered Annie telling her how Elizabeth always knew everything that went on in the casino. Maybe Elizabeth could help.

Stealing one more glance at her mother's picture, Debbie headed toward Elizabeth's office.

* * *

Dan parked in front of the two-story house and stared at the numbers. This couldn't possibly be Annie's house, not unless maids were being paid a lot more now-a-days. He retrieved his pocket notebook and double checked the address. They matched.

Maybe I should change jobs, he thought. He noticed that a light was still shining through the downstairs window. He rang the doorbell.

An elderly lady with solid white hair framing an oval, wrinkled face, which reminded Dan of a slightly deflated balloon, answered the door. She eyed him suspiciously, "Are you here about Annie?"

"Yes. I'm Dan Springer." He took out his wallet and showed her his press card.

"I'm Sue Lynn Kapetzy," she said opening the door wide enough to allow him to enter. "Is Annie all right?" She placed her opened hands on her chest as though guarding herself from the answer.

Dan pondered the question. "Why would you ask that?"

"Well, you're here, aren't you?   And whenever a policeman shows up, that means bad news." Sue Lynn wet her lips.

"A policeman?"

"That's who you are, right? A policeman? You showed me your badge."

"I'm a reporter. I showed you my press card."

"Oh." Sue Lynn stopped and gave a weak smile. "My eyes aren't what they used to be." She led him to the living room and pointed to the couch. "So why are you here?"

"I came to see Annie."

"Then you made a trip for nothing. She's not here." She folded her arms in front of her and sat down.

"Are you her roommate or a relative perhaps?"

"What if I am?"

"Ms. Kapetzy, it's very important that I speak with Annie. Can you tell me when you expect her or how I can reach her?"

Sue Lynn's lip began to quiver, and she wrapped her arms tighter around herself. "What do you want with her? Is she in some kind of trouble?"

"I hope not, but it's very important that I speak with her. Can you help me?"

Sue Lynn shrugged. "Don't see how. Annie's not here and I don't know where she is." She ran a trembling hand across her lips.

"You're worried about her, aren't you?"

Sue Lynn looked away.

"I'm also concerned about her. Maybe if we talk, we can find out where she might be."

Sue Lynn nibbled on her lower lip and stared at the

floor.

"Mrs. Kapetzy, I'm not the enemy. I'm here to help Annie, but I can't do it alone. Won't you help me?"

Sue Lynn kept her eyes glued to the floor.

"All right, at least tell me if I'm in the right track. Annie is Colette's mother, right?"

Sue Lynn's eyes popped opened like two huge buttons. "What-- Why--" She cleared her throat. "As long as I've known Annie, she's been telling these fantastic stories. She claims to have been Mr. Lovingsworth's mistress. And I'm the queen of England!" Even though her words were strong, her voice quivered.

Dan frowned. "Look, I know you're trying to protect Annie, but she doesn't need protection from me. She may very well be in danger and if she is and you don't help me and anything happens to Annie, you'll blame yourself for the rest of your life."

Sue Lynn remained sitting down, her head hanging low as big tears ran down her cheeks.

Dan waited for a while but when Sue Lynn didn't say anything, Dan stood up. "Fine. There's no need wasting my time, not when two people's lives may be in danger."

"Two?" Her voice was barely above a whisper.

"Yes, Annie's and Debbie Gunther's."

Sue Lynn gasped.

Dan went over to Sue Lynn and squatted in front of her. "You know Debbie Gunther?"

Sue Lynn shook her head. "No. No. She doesn't exist. It was just a joke."

"What was a joke?"

"The. . .the. . .dre--" She shook herself. "Nothing."

"The dress! You were going to say the dress. Annie asked you to call the casino seamstress to ask her to duplicate the dress Colette wore the night she died. And you did it, didn't you? You even told the seamstress that your name was

Debbie Gunther."

For a flash of a second, Sue Lynn's eyes met Dan's then she looked away. She sank deeper into the couch.

"And that's not all," Dan said. "She also had you order some flowers under the same name." Dan stood up. "But why? Why would she have you do that?"

Sue Lynn pouted and remained quiet. She played with the sides of her robe, folding it and unfolding it in a nervous gesture.

"Even now you won't help me? I swear, Mrs. Kapetzy, that if anything happens to Debbie, I will personally hold you responsible. Remember, I represent the press and that's a mighty persuasive tool. You will go to jail as an accessory to murder."

For a while Sue Lynn was quiet and Dan knew he had failed. He turned to leave.

"What do you want to know?"

Dan stopped and turned. "I want to know what you know."

"You're right. Annie is Colette's mother. That would make Colette Ms. Elizabeth's sister. Now, I don't know any of the details, but for some reason Ms. Elizabeth had Colette killed. She got away with it, but Annie swore revenge."

"How does Annie plan to get her revenge?"

Sue Lynn shook her head.

"Mrs. Kapetzy, I know this is hard on you. But time is ticking away. Every second I spend here with you, I could be spending saving Debbie's or Annie's lives."

Sue Lynn nodded. "I know. I'm sorry. But like you said, this is hard." She took in a deep breath. "Annie found a woman. Don't ask who. I don't know, maybe Debbie. Anyway, somehow Annie got Ms. Elizabeth to believe that this woman--Debbie?-- knew what really happened to Colette and was planning to expose Ms. Elizabeth's role in the murder."

"What did Annie plan to gain by this?"

"I guess Ms. Elizabeth was suppose to panic, and, to protect herself, she'd order this woman's death. Annie would then run to the police with all this evidence she'd accumulated. The police would come in, arrest Ms. Elizabeth, and as Annie often said, 'Justice was served'."

"That's a rather risky plan."

"I know." Sue Lynn ran her fingers through her thinning hair. "That's why I'm really worried. Annie always calls when she's going to be late, and she hasn't called. She's not at the casino, either. Do you think maybe Ms. Elizabeth got a whiff of what Annie was trying to do?"

"I don't know. What makes you think she's not at the casino?"

"Someone called from the casino about an hour ago. She wanted to talk to Annie, said it was important. She couldn't find her in the casino, but she was going to go look for her."

"Was it Debbie who called?"

Sue Lynn shrugged. "She didn't give a name, and I didn't ask. I worked in the casinos long enough to know I should never stick my nose where it doesn't belong. I wish Annie had done the same. She could be in danger."

So could Debbie, Dan thought. Without asking, he reached for the phone and dialed Debbie's number. There was no answer. "Damn!" He slammed the phone down. "I've got to get there as soon as possible."

Dan ran out of the house, his right hand fishing in his pants' pocket for the car keys. His mind constantly spoke to Debbie, *Please be all right. Please be all right.*

With a growing sense of dread, Dan decided to take the freeway as it'd be the most direct route. Once he reached the Strip, he'd make better time by taking the back roads. Luckily, most of the tourists were not aware these roads existed. He stepped on the accelerator, and his thoughts returned to Debbie. The speedometer needle climbed higher.

He knew he would feel foolish when he'd rush into Debbie's bedroom and like a noble knight rescue her--

--from a peaceful night's sleep

--from a bathtub filled with bubbles to calm her jittery nerves

--from...well, just about anything except any real danger.

Yes, he'd feel foolish, but at least he'd know she was safe because right now, he wasn't so sure. And until he was confident that Debbie was okay, he would continue to try to get to her as soon as possible.

He looked at the speedometer once again. It read seventy-seven. Surely, a few more miles an hour faster couldn't hurt.

Still thinking about Debbie, he zoomed past a parked car. Too late he realized that it belonged to a policeman, who by now, had probably already clocked him. Reacting on pure instinct, Dan slammed on his brakes in a futile attempt to slow down.

What Dan didn't take into consideration was that the Ford truck behind him was also speeding, and that its driver wasn't expecting the car in front of him to slow down so suddenly. Before Dan's mind could register all of this information, he felt his car jolt with the sudden impact of a bumper meeting another bumper.

Dan realized that it was a good thing he was wearing his seat belt because without it, he would have probably been hurled through the front window. As it was, the impact forced his body to sway forward with such brutal force that he hit his forehead on the steering wheel.

As he slowly raised his head, he realized he was skidding into the guardrails. He tried to correct his steering, but couldn't bring himself to do it. The world around him blurred, gradually turned gray, then a deep black.

Chapter 37

Elizabeth stood staring out the window of her office. The mountains surrounding Las Vegas were dry, sandy and desolate. It was a shame. All of the glitter Las Vegas had to offer would never change that.

Elizabeth sighed and turned her attention to Jack. "Is it done?"

Jack nodded. "Annie is dead."

"Good."

Jack started to leave.

"There's something else," Ms. Elizabeth said.

Jack stopped and waited for Ms. Elizabeth to continue. "How's Harry doing?"

Jack's body tensed. "He's lost two-hundred fifty thousand dollars." His eyes narrowed, watching for Ms. Elizabeth's reaction.

"And in the future?"

"He's part of the family again. Whenever he feels like gambling, I'm sure he'll come back to us."

"And it's all due to your bringing Debbie in."

Jack nodded and said, "He calls her Colette."

"You've done an excellent job."

Jack cocked his head as though listening carefully. "But?"

"Does he have any money in our cages?"

"A bit over one-hundred thousand dollars. In fact, one-hundred two thousand seven hundred and fifty dollars."

"Do you remember the Avery brothers?"

Jack searched his memory, then remembered. "Weren't they those con artists who tried to fool everyone by making a mold which resembled chips, then placing a real chip on top?"

"It sure looked like they had a lot of money, didn't it?"

Jack nodded. "It even fooled us for a while."

"Whatever became of those fake stacks?"

"They're locked away in the casino vault. I thought of sending them to the gambling casino museum."

"You'll do no such thing. What you will do, instead, is replace most of Harry's chips--the ones he plans to take home--with those fake stacks."

Jack let out his breath in an audible hiss. "If he finds them--"

"You make sure he find them."

"He'll think the casino is trying to cheat him out of his money." Jack ran his fingers through his hair. "Ms. Elizabeth, I worked very hard to bring him back. I did it for the casino."

"You did it for yourself." There was no trace of anger in her voice. She had simply stated a fact. "You want to become the general manager because it's the most powerful official position --that is, right next to mine. You and Thomas Buller have been running a neck to neck race for that job. All you needed was something that would put you just one step ahead of Thomas Buller. You found that something in the Harry/Debbie business deal."

"Regardless of my motives, Ms. Elizabeth, you must admit that it benefitted the casino--and that's the important part."

"I couldn't agree more, Jack. You showed initiative and I like that. That's why the position is yours."

It took a long second before her word fully registered in Jack's mind. "I got it?" he asked incredulously.

"I'll make it official tomorrow, provided Harry finds the fake stacks of chips. I hate to lose his business, especially after all the hard work you did to bring him back."

For a moment Jack was quiet. "You're going to have Debbie killed."

"She's a menace, Jack. She sent herself those flowers. Then there was that cute trick with the dress. Supposedly, she even knows about Waltman Park. Whatever game she's playing, I don't like it. She's a threat to us."

Jack sighed. "Sometime tomorrow, Harry will find the fake stack of chips."

"Tomorrow is too late. I want it done today." Ms. Elizabeth walked away from the window and sat on the couch facing Jack. "Did you bring the pills?"

"Yeah, Placidyl." Jack reached into his pocket and handed them to her.

"Tell me about them," Elizabeth said as she stuffed the pills into her pocket.

"They're sleeping pills--by prescription only. They induce sleep anywhere from fifteen minutes to one hour after consumption. They come in a soft white capsule and when its contents are squeezed into a drink, it tastes slightly alcoholic. Is there anything else you'd like to know?"

Elizabeth shook her head.

Jack walked over to the TV monitoring unit. He pressed three buttons. The television changed from the casino scene to Debbie's suite. It was empty. "Is that who the Placidyls are for? Debbie?"

Elizabeth nodded. "It'll look like suicide."

"What will her motive be?"

"The poor girl cracked under all the pressure. She simply couldn't handle it."

"Opening night, you mean."

"Partly that." Her eyes drifted toward the TV screen showing Debbie's suite. They remained there for a long time. She sighed deeply and said, "Did you know that she claims that there's a man who is stalking her?"

"Yes, Annie told us."

"Isn't that enough to drive a person to suicide?"

"I see what you mean." Jack changed the channel back to the casino. "Who's going to do it?"

"I will."

Jack's wide, unblinking eyes stared at Ms. Elizabeth. "Why you?"

"Debbie came after me, all sweet and innocent. She didn't think I would see through her obvious disguise. She's not that good of an actress. I want the satisfaction of doing this myself."

"Is that really wise?"

"Are you questioning me?" She felt her lips tight with suppressed anger.

Jack threw his arms up in the air as though surrendering. "I'll hang around the casino just in case you need me." He walked out.

Robert Howard, the man in charge of security, knocked on Elizabeth's door. "I'd like to talk to you, Ms. Elizabeth."

Elizabeth glanced at her watch. Debbie should be getting back to her suite any minute now. Elizabeth wanted to drop in on Debbie, pretending that she wanted to congratulate her on her success. But first she'd have to get rid of the security guard. "I can only spare five minutes," she said, opening the door wider so Robert could come in.

"Thank you. I appreciate that," he said.

Elizabeth closed the door and led Robert to the couch. She stared at him, waiting for him to state his business.

Robert cleared his throat and said, "I'll get right to the

point. I know that tomorrow there's going to be a budget meeting, and I wanted you to know how I, as head of security, feel before you go to the meeting."

"Thank you, Robert, I appreciate your--"

Elizabeth's sentence was interrupted by a loud banging on her door. She wasn't expecting anybody this late at night. She quickly glanced at Robert. "Come in," she said.

The door slowly opened and Debbie stepped inside. She spotted Robert and apologized. "I'm sorry. I didn't know you were busy." She started to leave.

Well, I'll be damned, Elizabeth thought. Out loud she said, "No! Wait, Debbie. Come back." Then she thought how horrible Debbie looked.

Debbie's face had been drained of all color, and her once sparkling eyes were now dark and void of any expression. Her mouth was slack, and she seemed to walk as though she had suddenly been crippled by arthritis.

Immediately, Elizabeth ran to her side and led her inside. "My God! What's happened to you?"

Debbie eyed Robert, then turned so Elizabeth could hear her. "Everything's gone wrong."

What game are you playing? Elizabeth wondered. I suppose I will soon find out. Feigning concern, Elizabeth asked, "What happened?"

"It's--it's my...father." Debbie's voice was barely above a whisper--whether it was to keep Robert from hearing or because it was part of her act, Elizabeth wasn't sure.

"Your father?" This was going to be interesting. And she had to hand it to Debbie: she was putting on a pretty good show.

Debbie nodded. "He--"

"Wait. Not here, Debbie." Years of experience made Elizabeth recognize this golden opportunity. "There'll be too many interruptions. Let's go to your suite where we won't be bothered. We'll talk over a drink." She wrapped her arm around Debbie and began to lead her out. They stopped in front of Robert. "I will contact you early tomorrow, prior to the meeting," Elizabeth said. "Thank you for coming."

Robert stood up and shook Elizabeth's hand. "I appreciate that." He turned to Debbie. "Ms. Gunther, I hope things work out for you. Good night."

As Robert walked out, Elizabeth smiled. Robert had definitely noticed Debbie's distraught condition. His testimony would be of great value at a later inquest.

Chapter 38

"He's dead!" Debbie said once she and Elizabeth had reached her suite. Debbie's eyes were wide and empty. "Today I buried him. I finally buried him. After all of these years of hoping and wishing." A shuddering spasm racked her body. "Somehow I always knew this day would come."

"You're talking about your father," Elizabeth said.

Slowly, Debbie nodded.

"Tell me all about it," Elizabeth said as she stood up and headed for the bar. "But first, I'll make us some drinks. You look like you could use one."

As Elizabeth stood behind the bar, she reached into her pants' pocket and produced several white capsules. She squeezed each one into what was destined to become Debbie's glass. This is it. You're dead, Debbie, Elizabeth thought.

She looked up at Debbie. "What would you like?"

"Something mild," Debbie answered. Then added, "The hell with it. Make it something strong."

"Rum and Coke and rum and rum?" Elizabeth smiled at her own little joke.

"That's fine."

Elizabeth poured the rum, next the Coke. She stirred both drinks, but perhaps Debbie's a bit more than hers. She picked up both of them, walked back to the couch, and handed

Debbie her drink.

Debbie stared at her drink and set it on the coffee table.

Damn! I wonder if she suspects. Elizabeth took a long sip, hoping Debbie would do likewise. "I'm all ears," she said.

Debbie took a deep breath and slowly began to talk about her father. As the narration progressed, Elizabeth found that her attention often wondered off. Surely, this was an interesting --and tragic--story, but what did all of this have to do with Colette? When was she going to get to the real story?

When Debbie finished, she remained still, the perfect image of defeat. Her hands were clasped; her head, bowed; her back, arched.

"What happened after he left?" Elizabeth asked.

Debbie shrugged. "Nothing happened after he left. I just hope I'll never see him again!"

She's either the best actress in the world or she's telling me the truth, Elizabeth thought. For a few moments Elizabeth stared at Debbie, her mind analyzing and digesting all of the new information. Finally, Elizabeth decided that Debbie was telling the truth. The anguish in Debbie's eyes could never be duplicated by an actress. "I'm sorry to hear about your father," Elizabeth said. "He's a jerk and you deserve better."

Elizabeth realized that Debbie was feeling miserable and that's when the idea first entered her brain. If it worked, Debbie would not only kill herself, she would also leave a suicide note. "When I was a little girl, my father taught me an interesting game."

"What's that?"

"When I was mad or angry or hurt, he'd make me write everything down. Then I'd wrinkle that paper and throw it away. All of the time I'd tell myself that I was throwing my anger away. It worked. And I'd bet you, it would work right now. So, why don't you go get a piece of paper and a pen."

Debbie did as told and within a minute she was back.

"Write this," Elizabeth said. She smacked her lips, hoping that gave her an aura of helpfulness. She began to dictate: "Tonight my father came to me demanding some money. I have at long last realized that he never really loved me and indeed hated me. My heart--my life--is shattered. There is no more." She momentarily paused, took a deep breath and continued, "Now print in large block letters: THERE IS NO MORE. I HATE HIM-HATE HIM-HATE HIM."

Debbie's body shook with emotion. Her lips trembled as she re-read the note she had written. She underlined several times the last phrase which read: *HATE HIM.* She wrinkled the note, then threw it on the floor.

Beautiful, Elizabeth thought. It's just perfect. The police will walk in here later on tonight, find her dead, then they'll find the crumbled note written in her own handwriting. Naturally, they'll assume it was a suicide note. "Feel better now?" she asked.

Debbie shrugged.

Elizabeth walked over and sat beside Debbie. "Just as you crumbled that note, you crumbled all feeling for your father. Agreed?"

Debbie nodded and in spite of her grief she managed to smile--a true, genuine smile that spoke louder than words themselves. Elizabeth looked away.

"Thank you, Ms. Elizabeth, I'm surprised at how well that works." She reached for her drink. "Let's toast to the fact that, as far as I'm concerned, my father is dead and buried. Let's drink to the ending of bad memories," Debbie said, raising her glass for a toast.

Chapter 39

"Are you sure you're all right?" the policeman asked.

For the past half-hour, Dan had been sitting on the curb while the policemen questioned him and the truck driver. At first Dan had felt disoriented, but now, aside from a pounding headache, he was feeling fine. "Yeah, I'm okay."

"You sure now?" The policeman glanced at the paramedics. The truck driver had broken his arm and suffered a possible concussion. The paramedics were in the process of loading him into the ambulance. "I can call them. Have them look at you."

"They've already done that. I signed a release form stating that I refused medical attention." Dan looked at his watch, and the vise in his stomach turned a notch. It'd been almost an hour since the accident and Debbie--what of Debbie? Was she in danger? No, or maybe yes. A chill invaded his body.

"You're lucky."

Dan looked up. "What?"

"I said you were very lucky. I've seen other car accidents which weren't as bad as yours and the people were killed."

Dan stood up. "Yes , I'm very lucky, but I'm also very late. May I go?"

"Yeah, you can go, but remember, luck like this doesn't last. Your car is a bit messed up, but it's still driveable and you weren't really hurt. Drive more carefully next time."

"I will, Officer." He snatched his speeding and reckless driving tickets in the glove compartment. "Remind me to pay them sometime."

"Yeah, sure," the policeman said.

Once again, Dan glanced at his watch. "I'm very late for an appointment. Where's the nearest phone?"

"Not this exit, but the next one down, take it. You'll see a Dunkin' Donut. There's a pay phone there."

Dan thanked him and drove off. Less than five minutes later, he was dialing Debbie's number.

On the third ring, he heard the phone being picked up. He recognized Debbie's voice. "Debbie! Thank God. Are you all right?"

"Of course, why wouldn't I be?"

"I'm not sure, but you may be in danger. Without letting anyone know what you're saying, I need to know some things. Will you be able to answer me?"

"Of course."

"I need to know if you're alone. Are either Ms. Elizabeth, or Jack, or Annie with you?"

"Why yes, an interview tomorrow at one would be just great."

"Interview at one?" Dan thought for a minute. "Oh, I see, you're trying to tell me that the first person I mentioned is there with you. That was...Ms. Elizabeth."

"You got it!"

"Listen, Debbie, I may be all wrong with this, but I have reason to believe that she may be dangerous. I don't want to explain now, but get rid of her now. If you can't, go down to the casino or any place where there's a crowd. I'm on my way over there now. I should be there in about ten-to-fifteen minutes. Will you be all right?"

"I think so. I'll look forward to that interview tomorrow."

* * *

Debbie hung up the phone and turned to face Elizabeth. "That was Dan. He wants to meet me tomorrow at one for an interview. I thought he was all through interviewing me, but apparently not. I'm glad though. I think he's cute."

She realized she was rambling, but she was trying to buy time. "Maybe he heard about my dad, huh?"

"Maybe," Elizabeth said, "which reminds me. We were about to toast to new beginnings." She picked up the glasses and handed Debbie hers.

Debbie reached for it. "If we're going to toast to new beginnings, let's do this right. Let's go down to the bar and we'll toast down there. I feel like submerging myself in Colette's world and forgetting about Debbie and her problems." She set the drink down.

"That sounds fine with me, but I have never been one for wasting anything." She raised her glass and looked at it. "This looks like a perfectly good drink to me. Let's finish these drinks first, then we'll go downstairs."

Reluctantly, Debbie reached for her drink and touched Elizabeth's glass with hers in a toast to the agreement.

Chapter 40

Jack spoke into the walkie-talkie. "CP 1, come in please. CP 1." Jack waited. Again, there was no response. It'd been more than half-an-hour since Ms. Elizabeth had gone with Debbie to her suite. Yet, a toast took what--five, ten minutes maximum? Surely, Debbie was dead by now and Ms. Elizabeth--what had become of her?

Jack felt the worry frown form on his forehead as he entered Elizabeth's office and turned on the surveillance cameras console. If Elizabeth was anywhere in the casino, Jack would be able to find her.

The first camera scanned several hallways. There were people coming and going. Jack glanced at their faces, their backs. Elizabeth was not among them. Jack turned his attention to the camera focusing on the casino table area. The two and five dollar black jack tables were filled to capacity. The cocktail waitress was delivering complimentary drinks to the two players playing on the twenty-five dollar table. Jack looked at all the customers and employees. Elizabeth was not with them. Another camera covered the curio shops and all of the restaurants. As usual, the restaurant offering the buffet was the fullest, but the others were by no means empty. Again, Jack failed to spot Ms. Elizabeth.

Another camera swept over the general casino. All of the nickel machines and most of the quarter machines were being used. Several dollar machines didn't attract a single gambler and all of the five dollar machines stood silent and lonely. Jack made a mental note to plant someone on the five dollar machines. Someone winning a big jackpot always attracted other hopeful gamblers.

Jack was about to press the button to change the angle of view when his eye caught something unusual. He wasn't sure what he had seen so he reached for the control button. The third camera re-scanned the same area. When he found it, he made the camera stop and focus on the aisle between the one-hundred dollar slot machines. Right there in the middle of the area, a figure was pushing his way through the crowded casino floor. That was what had attracted Jack's attention.

The man was walking fast, almost running. Whenever someone stood in his way, he moved clumsily around them. Often, he just simply pushed forward, causing several people to stare at his rudeness.

Jack zoomed in on the hurried man. It was Dan.

"Damn you, Ms. Elizabeth. It was foolish to get personally involved. I should have never let you do this," Jack said to no one in particular. With apprehension tightening his chest, he ran out of the office, not bothering to turn off the console.

He would follow Dan.

* * *

In the few seconds that it took Debbie to touch her glass against Elizabeth's, her mind spun with questions. Mustering all the courage she had and without the slightest hesitation, Debbie aimed the contents of her drink in Ms. Elizabeth's face.

Taking full advantage of Elizabeth's stunned reaction, Debbie shoved her would-be-killer. Without turning back to look, she dashed out the door and into the hallway.

She raced to the elevator and glanced at the numbers above them. The first one was on the second floor--the casino floor--but the second elevator was slowly climbing toward her floor.

She pushed the down button, willing the elevator door to open. She glanced back to see if Elizabeth was following. The hallway remained deserted. Why hadn't Elizabeth come? Because she was calling security. When the elevator door opened, it'd be crawling with security men.

Debbie made a ninety degree turn and headed down the hallway. Soon she found the EXIT stairway.

She reached for the door handle. It wouldn't budge. Surely it wouldn't be locked. She forced herself to breathe in deeply. She tried the door again. This time it opened effortlessly.

Debbie was half-way down the stairs when she saw a shadow ready to make the curve and head her way. She stopped, held her breath, and waited.

It was Jack.

"Oh, God!" Debbie said and covered her mouth with the palm of her hand. She turned around and headed up the stairs. Behind her she could hear Jack's fast footsteps steadily narrowing the distance between them.

Realizing she didn't have many options left open, Debbie headed back to the elevators, praying that they were clear of security guards.

Debbie made a right turn and headed down the hall where the elevators were. Please be empty, she prayed.

Debbie hastened her step, but came to a sudden stop when she saw the elevator door slide open. *They're here: the security!*

Dan stepped out. Their eyes locked.

The relief she felt was palpable, but short-lived. She

heard Jack close behind her. "Dan," she yelled, "hold the elevator!"

Dan pivoted, but the doors had already closed. He pushed the up and down button simultaneously, but to no avail.

The distance between Jack and Debbie narrowed so much that she could almost feel his hot breath on her neck. Debbie screamed.

* * *

It took Dan less than two seconds to surmise the situation. Propelled strictly by fear and an overwhelming desire to save Debbie, he grabbed Debbie's arm and yanked her toward him.

He stood protectively between Debbie and Jack, who by now had actually slowed down and seemed to be physically and mentally preparing himself.

Dan watched with morbid fascination, sprinkled with fear. From behind him, he barely heard Debbie say, "He's got a black belt in karate."

And then Dan knew what Jack was doing and all he could say was, "Ooooh shiiit!"

For Dan, time moved in slow motion. Although logic told him that no more than ten seconds could have possibly passed since he stepped out of the elevator door, he felt as though several hours had dragged by.

And suddenly he was in the past. Linda--the only woman, besides Debbie, he had ever loved--was dead. The police were there, but they weren't there to talk to him about Linda. "I'm sure they will come for you too," the police lieutenant told him. "And when they do, you're going to have to fight them."

His wife was dead, his baby was missing. Nothing else mattered. "I'm not a fighter."

"In that case, you'll have to learn how to fight dirty."

Fight dirty.
FIGHT DIRTY.

The words repeated themselves in Dan's mind like an endless tape. Dan knew if he was to defeat Jack, he would have to fight dirty.

"Get out of the casino! Go get help," Dan ordered Debbie without turning to look at her. What the hell had the policeman taught him about fighting dirty?

Make the first move. You'll catch him by surprise. Make it smooth and make it good. That'll probably be the only chance you'll ever get.

Dan positioned himself, but it was too late. Jack, with his years of karate experience, was very swift. Dan saw Jack's right foot rise toward his stomach. Dan knew the contact would send him sprawling back and possibly put him completely out of commission.

So Dan did the only thing he could. He slid to the right, but not fast enough. Dan caught the kick on his left shoulder. The pain brought bolts of lightning to his arm.

Never let the bastard know you're in pain. You're in control. Take hold of yourself and fight--fight dirty.

Even though Dan's shoulder roared in pain, he tried to ignore it and instead focused on Jack. He noticed that he had fallen several feet away from Jack, and now Jack was coming at him with a shit-eating grin on his face. A grin that proclaimed victory even before the defeat.

The grin both terrorized and somehow strengthened Dan's resolve. He waited until Jack got closer then kicked him in the groin, the way the policeman had taught him.

Jack grunted in pain, and his eyes popped open in surprise.

Once he's hurt, hurt him again. And do it fast. Remember timing is of great importance. Don't waste even a second.

Although the pain from Dan's shoulder shot through every nerve he had, Dan stumbled to his feet. He headed toward Jack who was doubled over, clutching himself.

Mastering every ounce of strength he had, Dan slammed his knee into Jack's face.

Whatever you do, make sure you finish the bastard.

Dan side-stepped Jack and with an open palm--not a clenched fist as the policeman had taught him--hit Jack on the base of the neck with the side of his hand.

As Jack fell face-down on the floor, Dan thought it was rather appropriate that it was a karate chop that felled the champion.

Make sure that he's out though. Never assume anything. Kick the bastard when he's down, but don't kill him. That'll only bring you trouble.

Dan decided not to kick him--just to get the hell out of there and somehow find Debbie.

Dan, not used to all of the strenuous exercise, breathed hard and through his mouth. He was about to head for the elevator when one of them swung open and two security guards stepped out.

"Ooooh shiiit!" Dan said. He held his wounded arm next to his body and headed for the stairs.

Chapter 41

Fear, apprehension, and uncertainty enveloped Debbie as she entered the elevator and stared at the floor numbers. Second floor: the casino, probably swamped by security. First floor: enclosed garage area, probably also covered by security. Third floor: motel rooms, all containing phones. She pushed the third floor button.

She watched the numbers on top of the elevator door slowly change. Nine. Eight. Only five more floors. Seven. Six. The elevator stopped, and Debbie's heart did a flip-flop. The doors slowly slid open, and Debbie pushed herself all the way against the wall as though that would provide some protection.

She waited.

And waited.

No one stepped in.

Coming out of her stupor, she immediately pushed the close button and the elevator continued its descent. Debbie breathed a sigh of relief.

Stupid! Stupid! Stupid! Debbie scolded herself. She should have gotten off on the sixth floor. It was free of security--or at least the elevator area was.

Again, the elevator stopped. This time on the fourth floor. Debbie held her breath.

A man dressed in a business suit stepped in. He barely glanced at Debbie then gave her his back. He pressed the button for the second floor. The elevator doors slid closed, and Debbie concentrated on the steady humming of the elevator's motor.

Just one flight down and she'd be--

The man turned around and grinned. "Miss Gunther," he said, "won't you do me the honor of accompanying me?"

In his right hand, he carried a gun. It was pointed directly at Debbie's heart.

* * *

Dan's inner voice propelled him down the stairs and encouraged him to keep going. *I've got to make it to the casino. There, I could get lost in the crowd. Then I can find Debbie.*

I've got to find Debbie.

The piercing pain in his shoulder came with a sharp, striking suddenness, causing him to clinch his teeth. He knew the pain was forcing him to slow down. He cursed himself for allowing it to do so.

The footsteps behind him drew closer. Dan, knowing he was in no condition to fight the pursuers, pushed himself to his limit. He increased his pace. With his injured shoulder, he knew he didn't stand another chance of winning a fight. Besides, these guys were probably armed. His only chance was to reach the casino.

Then he heard it.

Footsteps coming up the stairs.

Footsteps going down the stairs.

He was trapped. His only choice was to leave the stairway. He reached the fourth landing and threw the door open.

Even though he didn't take the elevator, he stopped long enough to push the down button. He then dashed toward the other set of stairs.

A second bolt of pain shot through him. He ignored it and concentrated on reaching the casino floor.

He made a sharp turn and saw the EXIT sign. He swung the door open and bounded down two or three steps at a time. He ran past the door leading to the third floor. Only one more level before he reached the casino floor.

Above him a door opened. His pursuers, he was sure. No matter. He could see the door leading to the second floor. It was only five stairs away. He had won. A small victory, but at least a victory. He opened the door and stepped into the casino.

Directly in front of him three security guards headed his way. To his left, four more. He had no choice. His only option was to head to the right, toward the tables where the casinos were usually congested.

The security people would grab him, Dan knew, and no one would help him. Everyone would assume he had done something wrong. Still the casino would not want an incident. The crowd was his best choice.

He had taken but a few steps when he spotted more security men. This time, they were coming toward him. And from behind him. Security guards flanked his right and left sides.

There was only one way left: up. But how? Wildly, his eyes searched, then froze when he realized that all the security men had stopped. All of their eyes were glued, not on him, but directly behind him.

Preparing himself for the worst, Dan turned around and felt all hope drain out. Jack, a bit bloodied but very much alert, stood staring at Dan. His eyes were blazing with hate.

"Nice of you to come," Dan said for lack of anything else

to say. He knew that all the dirty fighting he'd been taught couldn't possibly help him now. He'd only wish he'd been able to help Debbie.

"Hey, Dan!"

"Springer."

"Hey guy!"

"Daaan."

"Buddy."

Startled, Dan--and the security--turned to see who called him.

Leading the pack of reporters and photographers was Nathan Branson, Dan's rival reporter from a competing journal. "What's the scoop, Dan? You didn't think we'd find out. But we're here."

Under any other circumstances Dan would have been furious that the other reporters had gotten hold of his private scoop. But today, he could almost kiss Nathan and more than likely "Stan the Man" for enlightening the press.

"Nathan, my friend!" Dan said, motioning him as well as the rest of the reporters and photographers to join him.

Friend? Nathan momentarily stopped, a puzzled look on his face. "Friend? Who are you trying to con?" His eyes popped open when he noticed Jack Armstrong. "What happened to you? What's going on?"

Jack reached for his walkie-talkie and using a hushed but firm voice, he spoke into it. "This is CP 3A. Ease off. Repeating: ease off." He turned it off and returned it to his pocket. "Gentlemen, ladies," he said in a loud voice as the cameras flashed, "we all know this is not a very good place to take pictures or talk. Let's go up to my office where your colleague, Mr. Dan Springer, and I can answer all of your questions." He was all smiles, but his eyes contained a fierce glow when they bore into Dan.

A reporter stepped in between Dan and Jack. Dan

inched backwards. Another reporter rushed in to fill the space. Dan took several steps backwards. More reporters stepped in. Soon, Dan could no longer see Jack.

He quickly turned to his right and slid between the rows of quarter poker machines.

Chapter 42

"CP 1," blurted the male voice on the walkie-talkie.

Elizabeth immediately picked it up. "Go on," she said.

"We've picked up your merchandise, and it's ready for delivery."

"You were rather slow. What was the hold up?"

"There was a third party involvement. But CP 3A reports all is under control."

"In that case, bring the merchandise in." Elizabeth set the walkie-talkie down. Third party involvement. Probably Dan. She'd have to deal with him later.

But for now, she'd concentrate on finishing Debbie. Moving rather quickly, Elizabeth prepared another set of drinks, loading one with Placidyl. She was stirring it when she heard a knock on the door. "Enter," she said.

Debbie--her head held up high--entered first. Right beside her was the man Debbie had encountered in the elevator. Behind them was a security guard Elizabeth barely knew as Gene something or other.

"Well done," Elizabeth told both of them. She looked at the man who had found Debbie in the elevator. "And what is your name?"

"Christopher Queva."

"Well, Chris and Gene, expect a bonus in your paycheck this week." She nodded at Gene. "That'll be all."

Gene left and Chris positioned himself so that he blocked the front door.

Elizabeth turned toward Debbie. She recognized fear swimming in Debbie's eyes, but other than that, Debbie stood perfectly straight, her mouth pressed tight with defiance.

Elizabeth analyzed Debbie for a few seconds longer then said, "I'm afraid, Debbie, I under estimated you."

Debbie remained quiet, her eyes focused directly in front of her.

Elizabeth continued, "My mistake was assuming that because you impersonate Colette, you would be as shallow as she. But I was wrong. And believe me, I won't make the same mistake again." With her head she pointed to the two drinks she had prepared. "Let's toast to new beginnings."

Debbie glanced at the drink then back at Ms. Elizabeth. "No, thank you."

"Drink, I said," Elizabeth repeated.

"I'm not really thirsty."

"But I'm afraid you have no choice." Elizabeth nodded at Chris.

He stepped forward, retrieved a hand gun from his pocket and pressed the barrel against Debbie's temple.

Debbie sucked in her breath but didn't move.

Chris cocked the gun.

"Drink," Elizabeth ordered.

Debbie shut her eyes and swallowed hard. "I can't move. The gun," she said.

Elizabeth nodded once, and Chris stepped back, withdrawing the gun, but not putting it away.

Debbie opened her eyes and took baby steps toward

the bar.

"Pick it up."

Debbie's trembling hand reached for the glass. Several drops spilled to the floor. Debbie stared at the drink sloshing in the glass.

"Drink it!" Elizabeth nodded at Chris who immediately pointed the gun at Debbie's face.

Debbie flinched. "I--I won't."

"Shoot her," Elizabeth ordered.

Chris pulled the trigger.

The chamber was empty.

Debbie's legs buckled under her, and she steadied herself by reaching for the bar. Elizabeth smiled. "Have you heard of Russian roulette? That's what we have here. Five empty chambers and one fully loaded chamber. What do you think are your chances that the next one won't be the loaded one?"

Again she nodded, and the bodyguard cocked the gun. "Now drink!"

Debbie's hands were shaking so violently that when she brought the drink close to her lips, she spilled almost half of its contents.

"Drink!"

Debbie dropped the glass. The glass scattered. "Ooops. Clumsy me."

Elizabeth frowned. "That was really very stupid, Debbie. I had assumed that being the bright person you are, you would have preferred the drink. You simply feel sleepy, and you go to sleep. No pain." Elizabeth walked around and stood in front of her. "A bullet, on the other hand, is very painful. Your insides literary explode and you feel every inch of it."

"I really don't think you give a damn about my suffering. What I do think is that you want me to drink your poison so I won't mess up your little scheme. The drink could be explained as an accidental overdose or even a suicide. A bullet--well, that would be a lot harder to work into a suicide angle. Am I right?"

Elizabeth glared at her. "You're absolutely right, but what you keep forgetting is that this is my casino. I have professionals working for me. You wouldn't be the first person to disappear. Your body shows up with a bullet between your eyes, the police will investigate. They'll come to us, but they'll never be able to trace it to us. Remember we're the ones who did Colette in, and she was a much bigger star than you." Elizabeth paused and stared at Debbie. "So which is it going to be?"

"Do you really expect me to help you make it look like a suicide?"

Elizabeth sighed. "As you wish." She turned to Chris. "Shoot her."

He cocked the gun.

Debbie cringed.

Chris pulled the trigger but again the chamber was empty.

Fear almost caused Debbie to plummet to the floor, but sheer will forced her to remain standing.

Ms. Elizabeth shook her head in disgust. "You were lucky again, but you do know your luck diminishes with each round, don't you?"

Debbie didn't answer.

"Don't you?" Elizabeth repeated. When Debbie still refused to answer, Elizabeth said, "Fine, have it your way." Without looking at Chris, she ordered, "Shoot her!"

Chris raised the gun and took his time aiming.

"Wait!" Debbie's voice was high-pitched. "There is a third choice."

"I doubt that."

"If I die, the world will know what you did to Colette."

Debbie started speaking even before Elizabeth completed her sentence. "You're right. I have some evidence that proves your involvement in Colette's death."

Elizabeth raised her hand, telling Chris to hold on. "What kind of evidence?"

"Some pretty convincing evidence, and if I show up dead, certain people have instructions to release that evidence."

"Where is this evidence?"

"Not here. It's hidden. I'll tell you where it is, and you can go get it. Without it, I can't prove a thing. I'll give it all to you, but you'll have to promise me to let me go."

"Let me ask you something first. What were you hoping to accomplish by coming here? Were you going to blackmail me? Is that it?"

Debbie knew that the money angle would never work. She had to think of something else. "Yes, but not for money."

"Oh?"

"For fame. I knew you could open any door in Hollywood or New York for me."

"And now, what do you want?"

"My life. That's all."

Elizabeth seemed to consider this. "All right, but instead of telling me where this evidence is, you're going to show me where it is."

"No, you must let me go first."

"Why? So you can run to the police in the meantime? I don't think so. You're coming with us. If the evidence is what you say it is, you have my word. You will be released. If you're bluffing, then your death will be horribly slow." She pushed Debbie toward the door. "Now tell me, where are we going?"

Debbie searched her mind for the different possibilities. Banks had safety deposit boxes and at least one security guard who would hopefully help her. But banks would also be closed at this time of night. Ms. Elizabeth would probably choose to kill her rather than wait for a bank to open.

Chris reached for Debbie's arm and twisted it behind her. "Ms. Elizabeth asked you a question."

Debbie sucked in her breath as the bolt of pain traveled up her arm. "The main post office," she said. Chris released her arm, and Debbie massaged it. "It's in a P. O. Box I rented." She hoped the place was swarming with people.

Elizabeth went to Debbie's right side and Chris remained by her left. They pushed her along. "For your sake, you better be telling the truth."

Debbie momentarily closed her eyes and took in a deep breath. She felt the blood drain out of her body, and she knew that she was probably paler than she'd ever been before.

* * *

Dan glanced around him. The swarm of reporters had followed Jack into the elevator. Those who didn't fit ran for the steps. Their competitiveness had saved Dan and provided him with the opportunity to find Debbie.

Dan smiled at the irony. If they really wanted a scoop, they should be following him instead of Jack.

Now that he found himself alone, Dan kept a weary eye on the camera monitors and tried to move around the aisles he thought were safe. He headed toward the other set of elevators.

His thoughts focused solely on finding Debbie.

* * *

From the corner of his eye, Nathan watched Dan. He saw that the rest of the reporters were following Jack. Dan, on the other hand, was slowly working his way backwards. That meant that he was up to something. Nathan was willing to bet that whatever it was, it was certainly more interesting than anything Jack had to say.

He saw Dan step away from the crowd and with quick, jerky movements, he headed toward the back of the casino.

Nathan glanced at his colleagues and noticed that they weren't paying attention. He shrugged and followed Dan.

Chapter 43

For Debbie, the elevator's descent extended into eternity. Yet when its door swung open, Debbie drew back. What if no one recognized her? What if she couldn't spot a single person she knew? Would she then have to go with Elizabeth?

Elizabeth grabbed her arm and pulled her out. "Why are you hesitating, Debbie?"

"I didn't know I was." Except that she did know. She had no evidence, no place to take Elizabeth. She couldn't afford to leave the casino. If she did, she was dead.

The possibility left her cold and breathless. She had to gain control of her emotions, make Elizabeth believe she was in control.

Her eyes wildly searched the casino, hoping for an answer. She realized that she was now more than half-way through the casino, and still no one had stopped her. Her sense of foreboding deepened.

She could see the EXIT door. She sucked in her breath, took several hurried steps so she'd be in front of Elizabeth.

As though sensing something, Elizabeth also hastened her steps in order to keep up.

Debbie folded her arm and with all her might shoved her elbow into Elizabeth's stomach. Elizabeth, caught by surprise, exhaled a loud *whoo*. She held her stomach, the pain forcing her to bend over.

Debbie prepared herself to receive the blow she was sure Chris would administer. Instead, she was startled to see a figure come flying through the air and land on top of Chris. It was Dan.

The joy Debbie felt was short-lived. Several security guards were rushing toward her. Too late she realized that instead of watching them, she should have been taking care of Elizabeth.

Debbie felt an open palm hit her across the face so hard that the impact sent her bouncing several feet back.

Fury burned within her and fueled her will to survive. She leaped toward Elizabeth. Firm arms prevented her from reaching her.

She struggled to set herself free, but the two security guards--one on each side--firmly held her.

Dan met with the same fate. As soon as he landed on top of Chris, two other security guards yanked him to his feet. The pain shooting through his body was reflected in his eyes. He tried to favor his wounded shoulder, but his efforts were rewarded by a punch in the stomach.

"Everything is under control," a plainclothes security man said to the crowd who had gathered to watch. "Please return to the machines. The cocktail waitress will be there with free drinks. There's nothing else to see. These people will go to jail where they belong."

"It's not true!" Debbie shouted. "Someone please call the police."

"We are the police," the security man said. He flashed his badge at the crowd. "Now please move on."

"No! Please, wait. Help us," Debbie begged.

Other security guards came in and began to help disperse the crowd. Most people moved on, but a few stayed to watch.

Elizabeth turned to Debbie. "You bitch. You'll pay for this. You and your buddy are dead." She spoke loud enough for only Debbie to hear.

All hope drained from Debbie. She closed her eyes, fighting for strength. She felt the security guards drag her out of the casino.

Help us, her mind screamed, but she knew there was no one who could help.

* * *

A plain black car was parked in front of the casino. Its doors were wide open and several solemn-looking men stood staring through dull eyes at Debbie and Dan.

Debbie tried to free herself from the men's grasp. Beside her, Dan also struggled to get free. Neither of their efforts were successful.

Debbie and the security guards reached the car first. The men started to shove her in, but Debbie refused to cooperate.

"Not so fast," said a voice behind them.

Debbie's head swivelled toward the source of the voice. She saw a policeman, followed by several others heading toward her. Debbie's eyes then swept to Elizabeth.

Elizabeth glared at Debbie and back at the police. She rearranged her features into a smile and turned to greet the policeman leading the group. She stationed herself between them and Debbie.

"Officer, we're so glad you're here," she said. "We were just on our way to see Lieutenant John Champagne. We're handing these two people over to him. We got everything under control, but thanks so much for coming by."

Before Debbie could say anything, the security guard who flanked her right side placed his open palm on top of Debbie's head. He pushed down, thus forcing her to bend over. In the meantime, Chris, the other security guard, shoved her inside the car.

She was three-quarters in when she quickly glanced down. She spotted Chris's foot. Raising her own foot, she brought her heel forcefully down on top of Chris's.

"Damn fucking bitch!" Instinctively, he released the grasp on Debbie and tended to his foot.

Debbie wiggled her way out of the grasp of the other surprised security guard. She ran around Elizabeth and toward the policeman. "She's lying. She wants to kill us."

Elizabeth shook her head. "Office, surely you know me. I'm Elizabeth Lovingsworth, owner of this casino. As I told you, your lieutenant is waiting for us."

"Officer, does that sound like proper procedure?" Debbie asked. "If it was, would those two goons over there be holding Dan like that? You can see he's hurt, and they don't give a damn!" She pointed at Dan.

Dan's two security guards released him. Immediately Dan went to Debbie's side. The officer hesitated. The ones behind him waited to follow his lead.

"You do know the lieutenant?" Elizabeth asked.

"Of course."

"Then you know how pissed he's going to be when I tell him how you interfered."

The policeman seemed confused. He thought about it for a minute and slowly nodded.

Debbie formed a fist and hit the officer in the face. A bright red spot began to form where her fist met his face.

"Hey!" he said, rubbing his chin. The other policeman, guns drawn, bolted toward Debbie and Dan and quickly restrained them.

"Now you don't have a choice. You will have to arrest us, Officer," Debbie said.

Epilogue

"I can't believe you did that." Dan shook his head and smiled. He was leaning back on the couch in his living room, his right arm in a sling.

"What?" Debbie asked. She sat across from him on a single love seat.

"Hit that policeman like you did."

She shrugged. "Hey, it worked."

Dan smiled. "That it did. You're lucky he decided not to press any charges."

"He's lucky I decided not to press any charges. He almost left us in Ms. Elizabeth's claws."

She looked around Dan's living room. It was the opposite of what she imagined it would be like. She would have thought he was more of a hodgepodge man: a piece here, a piece there. Instead, the room was decorated with stark modern furniture with a lot of primary colors and chrome. A bright, abstract oil hung on the wall.

"It's not my style," Dan said as though reading Debbie's mind. "It was what my wife liked. So I kept it, kind of like a tribute to her."

"That's nice of you."

Dan nodded. "But useless. I've been living in the past.

I realize that now. I need to move on." He signaled for Debbie to come over.

She stood up. He patted the space beside him. She sat down, close to him.

"Debbie, I want you to know that I will never stop loving my wife, and I will never stop searching for my daughter. But that doesn't mean I can't love anyone else. Do you think you'll be able to live with that concept?"

She nodded and moved closer to him, resting her head on his good shoulder. He wrapped his arm around her, and they remained silent, each contemplating their own thoughts.

Dan hugged her tightly and Debbie looked up at him.

"A penny for your thoughts," he said.

"I was just wondering what you think is going to happen to Ms. Elizabeth."

"It's hard to tell. I know Colette's murder investigation is being reopened. That could mean trouble for Ms. Elizabeth, especially if Gladys testifies like she said she would. Also, we have all that information Annie gave us. Unfortunately, Annie won't be testifying."

"Do you think that'll hurt the case?"

"Most definitely, but then we'll make strong witnesses and hopefully that will compensate for the lack of Annie's testimony."

"Do you think they'll ever find Annie's body?"

Dan shook his head. "When the casino takes care of somebody, they take care of somebody."

Debbie sighed and closed her eyes, remembering Annie. She was quiet for a minute. "We were lucky the police showed up when they did."

"That was no accident."

"What do you mean?"

"Have you ever heard me mention Nathan?"

"Vaguely. Isn't he that reporter friend of yours?"

"He's more like my enemy, but I guess I shouldn't say that. He saved our lives."

Debbie stared at Dan. "How's that?"

"He's the one who called the police. He didn't know what was wrong. He just knew something wasn't quite right."

"Thank God for Nathan." She laid her head back on Dan's shoulder.

"Yes, thank God. Otherwise, you might not be here for me to hold you."

"Is that important to you?"

"Very much."

They were quiet for a minute before Debbie spoke again. "Do you want to hear something stupid?"

"Go ahead."

"This experience was actually beneficial."

"How's that?"

"I used to think that Debbie Gunther was a nobody. But when I came one inch from losing my life, I realized how much I wanted to live. I realized that I am a somebody, that everybody in one way or the other is a somebody."

"A very special somebody," Dan said. He lowered his face to meet hers. He stared into her eyes, then kissed her.

Also by
L.C. Hayden

Who's Susan?

Other novels from Top Publications

by
WILLIAM MANCHEE

Twice Tempted
Brash Endeavor
Undaunted
Death Pact

by

Lynnette Baughman

A Spy Within

Visit our website at
http://www.TopPub.com